"Finn..."

He waited, in silence, to see where that sentence was going. But it seemed Madeleine either didn't know or didn't want to share it with him, because her voice faded out. Her eyes dropped, too. To his lips, and then back up again.

Her lower lip slipped between her teeth and she bit down, and he knew that they were thinking the exact same thing. How would it feel to press his mouth against her lips? To feel the slide and the power of them beneath his own? To taste and to test? To press against her until they were stretched out on the grass?

The cry of a baby behind him brought a stifled groan to life, and Maddie took a breath as she glanced over at the stroller.

Maybe it was for the best, he considered, as he followed her gaze and saw Hart stirring.

And maybe he was going to spend the rest of the day wondering exactly where that look might have taken them if they hadn't been interrupted.

Dear Reader,

I don't think there's anything more adorable than a six-month-old baby. They're all rolly and cuddly and babbling and fun—but probably not yet mobile enough to get themselves into trouble while you're making a cup of tea.

They're also flipping hard work: the sleepless nights, the sterilizing, the trying to get all four of those wriggly limbs into a babygrow all at the same time, only to have to change it again ten minutes later.

It's gloriously intense, which seemed like the perfect backdrop for helping two people find each other. Because as long and dark as those nights pacing the corridors can be, when you're in it with someone you care for, making someone tea and toast at four in the morning looks a lot like love.

I hope you find as much joy in this story, these babies and this family as I did in writing it. I wish you many hours of unbroken sleep.

Love,

Ellie Darkins

Reunited by the Tycoon's Twins

Ellie Darkins

Recycling programs
for this product may
not exist in your area.

ISBN-13: 978-1-335-55624-0

Reunited by the Tycoon's Twins

Copyright © 2020 by Ellie Darkins

Harlequin Enterprises ULC
22 Adelaide St. West, 40th Floor
Toronto, Ontario M5H 4E3, Canada
www.Harlequin.com

Printed in U.S.A.

Ellie Darkins spent her formative years devouring romance novels, and after completing her English degree decided to make a living from her love of books. As a writer and editor, she finds her work now entails dreaming up romantic proposals, hot dates with alpha males and trips to the past with dashing heroes. When she's not working, she can usually be found running around after her toddler, volunteering at her local library or escaping all the above with a good book and a vanilla latte.

Books by Ellie Darkins

Harlequin Romance

Visit the Author Profile page at Harlequin.com.

For my girls

Praise for
Ellie Darkins

"Ellie Darkins brings two polar opposites together in this divine novel, where it's a clash of fierce emotions and beautiful, tender romance that warms your heart...engaging dialogue and skilled storytelling bring this story to life and capture your attention instantly!"

—*Goodreads* on *Surprise Baby for the Heir*

CHAPTER ONE

'MADELEINE, WHAT'S WRONG?'

Finn took in the scowling face of the woman on his doorstep and tried to reconcile it with the girl he had first met more than two decades ago and hadn't seen in more than two years. And then she let loose an impressive string of expletives and Finn's eyes widened.

This definitely wasn't the girl he remembered from his teenage years, loafing around her house with her brother.

He covered the ears of the baby he was snuggling on his shoulder, but the tirade came to an end and he breathed a sigh of relief, removed the emergency ear muffs and stepped aside so that Madeleine could follow him into the hallway of the townhouse, and then on into his apartment.

'Are you okay?' Finn asked, wondering

why Madeleine Everleigh had turned up on his doorstep fuming mad.

When his best friend Jake had talked him into letting his sister stay and help with the babies for a few weeks, he had thought that he was doing her a favour.

'An idiot in a white van beeped at me,' Madeleine said, following him into the apartment. 'It's nothing.'

No doubt she had to put up with this crap all the time. He'd known Madeleine for ever, and it had not exactly been possible to ignore that she was a woman with lush curves and a beautiful face, however hard he tried.

'It's not nothing; you shouldn't have to put up with that. I'm sorry it happened,' Finn said, shaking his head and wishing he could take back the last few minutes. 'Come through. I'll put the kettle on.'

The baby on his shoulder gave out a little squeak and Finn shushed him and bounced on the spot, only slightly frantically, hoping for just five more minutes before his son woke. He'd only been asleep for half an hour—if his routine went out then his sister's routine went out and then the rest of the day and probably the night would be complete and utter chaos. They'd all spent the three months since his ex-wife had moved abroad trying to build a routine, but losing his nanny when they'd only just settled into one again had thrown a spanner in the works and, without help, everything was at risk of descending into madness.

'Look, I appreciate it and everything but…' She cast a look at Hart that reminded Finn of how he had looked at babies before he'd found himself the single parent of two of his own. She was not exactly ideal nanny material, but he had promised his best friend that he'd give his sister somewhere to stay and a regular wage while she was between jobs. Jake hardly ever asked for favours and after twenty years of friendship it was really the least that Finn could do.

'This is Hart, by the way,' he said, giving the baby a gentle pat on the bum. 'Bella's asleep too, but this one is allergic to his crib.'

He laughed at the horrified expression on her face.

'Only metaphorically,' he reassured her. 'I've tried everything but a lot of the time he'll only sleep on me. Which is why I need the help.'

'Yeah, I don't know if Jake mentioned but I really don't have any experience with babies. I mean, his were all older than this when he adopted them.'

Finn smiled, and hoped it didn't look too forced. 'Yeah, he did mention it and it's fine, honestly. I just need an extra pair of hands for a few weeks until I can find a permanent nanny—I don't want to rush into hiring someone so it's great that you could help out at such short notice.'

Her face tightened, and Finn could have kicked himself for causing that reaction.

'Well, one of the great things about being fired,' Madeleine said, 'is that you can be super flexible. Really, I can recommend it…'

He reached his free hand towards her, then let it fall, realising he didn't know what he had been planning on doing with it. There was something about being around Madeleine that was making him feel like a kid again, and he couldn't say that he liked it. Everything that he had said in the last five minutes had been utterly the wrong thing and he didn't seem to be able to get off the back foot. And he'd invited her to stay, in his home, for at least a few weeks. He must be completely mad. 'I'm sorry, Madeleine. Jake told me that they made cutbacks at the website…'

'Yep.' She folded her arms across her body, and her expression went from irritated to full on angry. 'I don't know why I'm surprised. I escaped the last round, but everyone knows that there's no such thing as job security in journalism any more. I knew it was coming but it was still a shock.'

'Of course it was. It's a lot to take in. But is it too much of a cliché if I say that their loss is my gain? You're doing me a massive favour,' Finn said, smiling, hoping to ease her bad mood, 'and I truly appreciate it.'

She did smile at that, and he saw her shoulders relax a fraction. That was good; he wanted her to be comfortable here. He was hardly doing Jake a favour if his sister was so on edge the whole time that she was here that she couldn't even get through the door without worrying about him ogling her.

'You're the one giving me a place to

stay. I think you're the one doing the favour really.'

He didn't remember her being so prickly when they were kids. Of course she wasn't, back then. Nobody made it into adulthood without a major dose of reality to knock the idealism out of them. Or maybe that was just his divorce talking.

'Wait until the twins are both up at three in the morning. We'll talk then about who's helping out who,' he said with a wry smile. 'Anyway, can I take your bag? Let's go through to the kitchen—I'm desperate for caffeine—then I'll show you your room. Do you want tea or coffee?' he asked as he gestured for Madeleine to take a seat at the kitchen island, but she stayed standing.

'You sit,' she said. 'You've got the baby.'

He smiled. 'I've barely managed a sip of water all day so I'm not going to argue with you. See, this is working out perfectly already.' He watched as she grabbed cups from the top of the coffee machine, slotted in a pod and made a couple of espressos. He took one from her gratefully and she finally took a seat beside him.

'I'm sorry,' she said, as she drank half

the coffee in one go, then let out a long sigh as she relaxed back on her stool. 'I turned up in a bad mood and I shouldn't have taken it out on you.'

Finn smiled, grateful for the change in atmosphere. 'You've been through a lot. It's understandable.'

Madeleine quirked her eyebrows in a gesture that spoke of untold cynicism. 'None of it's your fault, though,' she said. 'You've already been better too good to me.'

Finn frowned. 'Don't say things like that. You deserve good things happening to you, Madeleine. I don't like that someone's made you think otherwise.'

He held her gaze for a moment too long, feeling the atmosphere between them grow heavy, and then Hart turned his head and nuzzled into Finn's shoulder, and he knew that they were on borrowed time.

'Could you take him while I make up a bottle?' he asked, and laughed at Madeleine's wide-eyed reaction. He chuckled softly as he transferred the baby into her arms. 'It's fine,' he said. 'Just bounce him a bit if he starts to cry. He's going to wake up hungry and that's not the best time to be showing you how to make up a bottle. We'll go through it all after.'

'Um, okay, I guess?' Madeleine said, bouncing the baby awkwardly in her arms. Finn laughed. 'Don't look so terrified, Madeleine. Jake said you didn't have much experience, but he didn't mention a mortal fear of children.'

'I'm not afraid!' Madeleine said with a flash of defiance that hit him straight in the gut. God, he liked that. But this was definitely not an appropriate thought to have about his best friend's sister. Or about his kids' babysitter for that matter. Temporary or not. He concentrated on the formula machine, pressing buttons and moving bottles on autopilot, until he had two bottles made up. If Hart was hungry, no doubt he would be hearing from Bella soon enough too.

With Madeleine taking care of Hart for a second, he allowed himself a moment to lean against the worktop and feel—really feel—how tired he was. If anything was going to distract him from his completely inappropriate thoughts about Madeleine, it would be that. Most of the time he managed to keep the fatigue at bay. But since his last nanny had left a week ago, he'd barely managed a minute's break.

His assistant was keeping the business ticking over, with him squeezing every minute of work into the day he possibly could, but there was only so long that that could carry on. He had built that business from the ground up and he wouldn't see it founder because he couldn't get proper childcare in place. With everything that the business had been through recently— their move to new premises, the enormous amount of money he had had to borrow to make that happen...

He had survived his divorce; he would survive this. But only if he stayed focused. Which was why he was so grateful that Madeleine had agreed to help him out. For the first time in weeks he could see himself actually getting back to the office some time this year, and without two babies strapped to him.

That was what he had to remember when he was tempted to sneak a look at her. When he was tempted to think of her as anything other than his best friend's sister or his temporary sitter. He and his business had survived the breakdown of his marriage by the skin of his teeth. They were still only surviving because he was generating enough income to service the debt that he had accrued in order to separate his and Caro's finances fairly and equitably. His company couldn't withstand any more disruption. His *life* couldn't stand any more disruption—he wasn't opening himself up to that again. Ever. So this sudden and inconvenient attraction to Madeleine didn't matter in the slightest.

He turned back to the kitchen island and smiled despite himself at the sight of Madeleine gazing thoughtfully at Hart. 'You two getting to know each other?' he asked, concentrating his gaze on the baby as the safest course of action.

'Babies are weird. He's a whole, real person,' Madeleine said, a little line creasing her brow. 'Only much, much smaller. And we don't know who he is yet. Don't you think that's a little strange?'

'A little,' Finn agreed. 'Don't worry. Spend enough time with them and you'll be too tired for philosophy.'

'You know you're really not selling this.'

'Too late,' he said with a laugh. 'You've already agreed.'

She rolled her eyes. 'I could change my mind.'

'And leave me in the lurch? You wouldn't. Jake would be mad.'

She huffed a little breath of a laugh. 'Aren't we a little old for threats like that?'

He smiled. 'Probably. Here, do you want to try him with this?'

She took the proffered bottle from him and stroked it over Hart's lips, then smiled down at him as he latched onto the teat, still only half awake. Madeleine beamed down at Hart, totally absorbed in watching him drink, and Finn forced down the warm feeling that was growing in his chest. It was just hormones, he told himself. It was natural to feel that when you were looking at a woman feed your baby. It was just nature. It didn't mean anything. It definitely didn't mean that he was interested in Madeleine because that would be more than inconvenient. It would be a complete disaster.

CHAPTER TWO

SO...BABIES ARE OKAY, really, Madeleine thought, as she looked down at Hart drinking his milk, eyes rolling back in his head and cheeks wobbling. *Yeah, babies are fine.* It was the dads that were the problem. Well, one dad in particular. This one, whose eyes she could feel on her as she fed his son.

She was used to feeling men's eyes on her. They followed her down the road, fixed on her in lifts. Judged her from across a desk at work. They scraped on her skin from the minute she left the house until the minute she locked the door behind her at night, breathing out a huge sigh of relief as she did so.

She felt Finn's eyes on her occasionally since she'd arrived. Only, they didn't scrape. They...nudged. Suggestively, enquiringly, in a way that she was actually in danger of enjoying.

With some coffee inside her, and the baby on her knee, she could feel the tension leaching from her muscles and the rough start to her day starting to fall from her. There was something about the rhythmic sucking from the baby that held her attention absolutely. It wasn't until the bottle was empty and Hart was sucking on air that she looked up from him to find Finn watching her.

His eyes were fixed on her face, never wandering south, and she felt her cheeks warm.

'See, you're a natural,' he said, taking the bottle and the baby from her and laying Hart on his shoulder.

'I don't know about that,' Madeleine said with a shrug. 'But I'm glad I can help out. Did your last nanny leave in a hurry? Jake didn't tell me much…'

Like how you found yourself a single dad in the first place, she thought.

One minute Finn Holton had been the high-powered CEO of a company bringing ground-breaking technology to the world on a regular basis. The next he had been photographed with twin babies in a sling, and his wedding ring nowhere to be seen. The tabloids had gone understandably silly at this turn of events, but no one seemed to really know what had gone on. And she should know how hard they'd tried.

Not being a reality TV star or other such worthy, Finn's story hadn't made it to her desk at work. And thank God no one at the website had known about the childhood connection between her and Finn, otherwise they would have been harassing her for details that she didn't have.

It might have saved her job, she thought for a second, if she could have dished some dirt on her brother's friend. But she had none to dish. Jake had told her nothing, and Finn was hardly likely to tell her anything either. He knew that she was a journalist. To be honest, she was surprised that he had let her into his home at all. She couldn't imagine that he was going to start spilling his guts to her.

If only he knew that she didn't have the least interest in his personal life. She'd never wanted a career in celebrity gossip.

But she'd left university without the double honours in politics and journalism she'd worked so hard for, and had found herself having to take any job she was offered. She'd thought the blog would be a stepping stone towards what she really wanted to be doing, serious political investigative journalism. But instead she'd found herself pigeonholed. Doors slammed in her face and job applications unanswered. So she'd written clickbait, filed her copy and gone home at night with the sensation that somehow she'd found herself living someone else's life.

When the last round of redundancies had been announced, she'd been relieved as much as she had been concerned. A redundancy would give her a chance to make a change in her career. In her life. That was until her landlord had given her an eviction notice the following week, and she'd realised that she wasn't going to be able to get a new flat without a regular source of income. If she decided to go freelance—scrabbling around for the same work as all her colleagues who had also just been let go—it would be years before she had enough of an accounting history to pass a credit check. When she had called her brother and whined on the phone to him, he'd told her he'd call her back with an idea—and he had.

Which was how she had found herself in Finn Holton's kitchen with a baby on her knee, wondering about the details of his personal life.

I mean, she shouldn't be curious. It was none of her business how one of the country's leading technology moguls, and wealthiest men, had found himself a divorced single dad. If he had been a single mum, no one would have given a second thought to the fact that he was the one raising the babies. But he wasn't a woman. And his situation *was* unusual. Which made her wonder.

Her career might have focused more on celebs falling out of nightclubs than on the business pages, but that didn't mean she didn't have a journalist's instincts at all.

'Jake was right, though. You're good at this,' Finn said as he put the baby down in the Moses basket in the corner. 'My children might be younger than his, but you've got the knack.'

'Must be an auntie thing,' Madeleine said. 'I've had enough practice with his brood. Who has four kids, really?'

'They are great kids, though.'

She smiled but could feel her eyebrows pulling together even as she did so. Finn was not what she had been expecting. At all. When she thought back to the kid she had seen occasionally in her kitchen at home, demolishing a loaf of bread's worth of toast with her brother as they messed about on her family's computer, there hadn't seemed much remarkable about him at all. She was pretty sure that she'd never paid him more than fleeting attention. I mean, who did, to their snotty little brother's mates?

If she'd known then the success that he was going to achieve, the enigmatic figure that he was going to become, would she have paid more attention?

Probably not, she admitted, letting her smile spread to her eyes. Teenage boys were unbearable. It didn't matter who they were going to grow up to be. She wondered if Finn remembered her as a teen-ager. Trying to swamp her emerging curves in giant T-shirts and baggy jeans. Whether he'd been one of the boys at school who had taken bets on whether they could sneak into the changing rooms while she was in PE and steal one of her bras.

No. Jake would have known. And he would never have allowed Finn in the house if that had been the case.

He looked nothing like the spotty, awk-ward-looking kid in worn-out trainers he had been then. She sneaked another glance at him while he was distracted by the baby, her journalist's eye taking a quick inven-tory, hitting the important points. Designer jeans, discreet but expensive watch, crisp white T-shirt, showing no sign of doing battle with two babies. Really, that wasn't fair. She was pretty sure her shirt had milk on it already and she'd only been here for an hour. But the clothes were all window-dressing, really.

It was the face that interested her. Be-cause you could change your clothes. You could drag yourself out of poverty and change your life and wear a new wardrobe. But you couldn't change your face. And when she looked at Finn, she could see him. The lost little boy who had spent more time in her family's kitchen than his own. Who had turned up starving, and had left stuffed to the gills with food by her mum, who'd known that he was probably going back to a cold house and an empty fridge. Who'd been packed off with clothes that Mum had just happened to find at the charity shop next door to her work, that wouldn't fit Jake and couldn't be returned.

He'd been a part of her family for years. But those years had happened to coincide with her later teenage ones, when she had spent as much time as humanly possible hidden in her room, avoiding her family. And anyone else for that matter.

Her teenage years hadn't exactly been a happy time, and being forced to revisit them, by virtue of the constant reminder that was Finn, hadn't been a part of her plan. But, as she had nowhere else to go, she was stuck with him, and the memories.

Finn was still making goofy faces at the baby, so she took another minute to look at him. To see the man, rather than the boy. There was no hiding from the fact that somewhere along the line he had become…beautiful. There was no other word for it. High cheekbones sloped down into a strong, stubble-covered jaw. Wide green eyes under dark brows, and a full mouth curved into a smile as he chatted gibberish to his son. It was a pretty picture. If you liked that sort of thing. And the warmth low in her belly was all the proof—if proof were needed—that Madeleine absolutely did like that sort of thing.

She wondered if it had all changed him. The money. The success. The business. Of course it must have changed him. But *how* had it changed him? she wondered. Had it made him hard? Had he had to become tough, in order to break the cycle of poverty, finish his education, start his business? If it had, she couldn't see it now, with the sunshine streaming in through the windows and a baby chuckling goofily up at him. But that didn't mean that it wasn't lurking somewhere under the surface.

It didn't matter, she told herself sternly. Because she was staying in his home, she was looking after his children, and what she thought about him personally was completely out of bounds. It didn't matter if he was beautiful. It wouldn't matter if he was tough. Because any sort of a relationship—even the shortest of flirtations, the most casual of flings—was completely off the cards.

And flings were the only sort of relationship that Madeleine could tolerate. Get in, have fun, get out before they could disappoint you. That was what ten years of working and dating in London had taught her. So she swiped right and accepted blind dates and chatted to guys in bars, always safe in the knowledge that she was going to cut ties before they had a chance to disappoint her.

And there was no question that she would always be disappointed in the end. She'd learnt that early on in her love life, before she had even left school. When it didn't matter how sweet the boy was or how interested he pretended to be in her life; all he really wanted was to get a hand in her bra. And ever since she had worked that out, she had been happier. She accepted that no one saw past her body and her face, and all the assumptions that they would make about her. And as long as she didn't expect more, she could have fun with them for a few weeks. Relationships happened on her terms, met her needs and ended when she decided. It had kept her bed warm and her evenings full since she had been in London, and she was happy with that.

Except...that would never lead to this, she thought, watching Finn with Hart. It didn't lead to marriage and babies and a family of your own.

But she didn't care about that, Madeleine reminded herself. Single dad of twins wasn't exactly a nuclear family either. Nor were her brother and his husband and their adopted brood. She had other options if she decided that she wanted a family one day. Options that didn't include pretending that the guys she hung out with were able to take her seriously enough to be interested in anything more than her body.

And that was before she even got started on her disastrous professional life, which had never recovered from her decision to quit university in her final year. Which had led to her not being able to get the political reporting internships that she had wanted, which had led to her being on the entertainment desk of a second-rate gossip website, which apparently hadn't been generating enough income from its clickbait to actually continue paying its staff.

She shook herself, physically as well as metaphorically, causing Finn to look over at her.

'Sorry, we were ignoring you,' he said with a smile. 'I got distracted.'

She smiled at the pair, who were really too cute to be real. She'd had no idea what the sight of a beautiful man with his baby could do to a girl's ovaries, but she was pretty sure she'd just popped out an egg. And just as rapidly shut down those responses. This was just hormones. And stress. And…something of a dry spell. She wasn't sure what else she should be blaming it on. It didn't matter what the reasons were; the only thing that mattered now was that she shut it down.

'It's fine. I get it. I'm here to help, so just let me know what you want me to do.'

'Will you watch him again for a few minutes?' Finn asked, glancing at the clock on the wall. 'I should really wake Bella. If she goes too far off his schedule then the whole day falls apart. Pick him up if he starts to grizzle.' Which he started to do the minute that Finn moved away from him.

'Of course,' Madeleine said, taking Hart on her shoulder and rubbing his back out of instinct. Finn looked at her for a moment, and she felt herself starting to blush.

'Jake was right. You really are a natural at this,' he said, and Madeleine met his eyes, surprised.

'Yeah, well, I'm the fun auntie. I have the easy job.'

Finn nodded, and Madeleine turned away, uneasy under his gaze. And a little embarrassed. She had assumed that he had been looking at her because, really, it was what she was used to. But of course he had been looking at his son.

Maybe Finn wasn't attracted to her. That would certainly make life easier. Make the spark of attraction that she had felt for him a little less inconvenient too. Except… she had seen the way he had occasionally looked at her since she had arrived. It definitely wasn't as brotherly as would be convenient for her right now.

She tried to think back to the times that their paths had crossed in her childhood home, long since sold so that her parents could pursue their adventures abroad. Had Finn ever looked at her with adolescent heat in his eyes? Had she ever thought of him as something other than her pain-in-the-butt brother's pain-in-the-butt friend?

Of course not. Thinking back to her teenage years, it was unlikely that she'd peeled her eyes away from the floor for long enough to even get a proper look at him.

It had taken a long time for her to work out that the way to stop people looking at her was to stare them down rather than avoid their gaze. She had an expression that she knew could shame even the most hardened of voyeurs from fifty paces. It had taken time and practice to perfect, but she'd had no shortage of opportunities.

The pad of footsteps behind her made her spin on her stool, and Finn reappeared with another baby on his shoulder, the white of her Baby-gro as fresh and clean as the cotton of Finn's T-shirt.

'This sleepyhead here,' Finn said, half

spinning on the spot so that Madeleine could see the baby's face, 'is Bella. Bella, say hi to Madeleine.'

Madeleine smiled at the baby, because who could resist a six-month-old, with their chubby cheeks and their chunky limbs, all energy stored up for crawling and walking and the chaos that was to come? But, for a little while longer, she would still be this gorgeous little chunk of babbling perfection, personality shining out of her, even when she was still half asleep.

'They're both so gorgeous. I don't know how you get anything done,' Madeleine said with a smile.

'I don't.' Finn laughed, though it sounded a little strained. 'That's why you're here. I think it would be a good idea if we all spent some time together over the weekend, get them settled in. Then next week I'll work from home but start building in a bit of time at the office. Get them used to it. Does that work for you?'

'*I* work for you,' Madeleine reminded him. 'It works how you want it to work.'

Finn narrowed his eyes at her. 'I'm not

thinking of it that way. You're not an employee, Madeleine. I don't want this to be weird.'

'It's not weird.' She shook off the suggestion, tried to pretend that she was completely comfortable around Finn. Not unsettled at all by the attraction she was feeling for him.

'Good, because I thought we were just friends helping each other out. I'm really grateful for what you're doing.'

'And I'm grateful too, for the place to stay.'

'Good. You know that Jake is like family to me, right. Which means you're family too. Which means I want to help you out. Okay? The fact that you're able to take care of the kids for a few weeks, and I'm able to make sure that you are fairly compensated for that, that doesn't change how I see this, okay? If there's anything you're not happy with, if you change your mind or you find a new flat next week and you don't want to stay, you just tell me, right?'

She nodded, forced a smile, but it didn't matter what he said; this was already more complicated than he realised.

CHAPTER THREE

SHE LOOKED TRAPPED, and he hated that look on her face. Her expression when she said that she worked for him, he hated that too. He wasn't sure what it was, that haunted, distrustful look that told him that not everyone she had worked for had treated her fairly. It reminded him of how she had looked when he had opened the door to her earlier, when she had been harassed by the driver of a van.

'So…dinner tonight,' Finn said, changing the subject. 'My housekeeper, Trudy, has gone for the weekend, and I usually fend for myself.'

'My goodness, such a modern man,' Madeleine said with an eye roll. 'I'm sure I'm very impressed.'

'Save it for the stand-up routine,' Finn said, grinning. 'Fending for myself usually involves ordering pizza. If you're nice to me, I'll let you share.'

'Wow. Those millions sure have made you generous.' She smiled, but then felt awkward, seeing the look on his face when she mentioned money.

'I'm still just me,' he said, his voice low and serious.

'I know,' she said and smiled, reassuring him. Even though, to be honest, she didn't really know him at all. But she knew entitled, privileged jerks when she saw them, and so far he didn't seem to be one. 'However fancy your kitchen gadgets. I like the apartment, by the way. How long have you been here?'

He produced a smile that didn't look quite natural. 'Since just before the babies were born. We sold the house when Caro and I…'

'Right, of course.' Madeleine tried to cover the awkward pause that inevitably followed accidentally bringing up someone's fairly recent divorce, not wanting to pry. But, at the same time, she was living with this man—albeit temporarily—and couldn't deny that she was curious about what had happened. I mean, she was only human.

'It was all very amicable,' he said, though a line had appeared between his eyebrows. 'We're still friends, of course. The twins, you know.'

Madeleine narrowed her eyes as she watched Finn. That all sounded too easy, and none of it explained the slightly pinched expression that he had assumed. The look of someone who had had too little sleep and too much worry in recent months, if she had to guess.

'It sounds like you were very grown-up about the split.'

Finn shrugged and gave a half-smile that came nowhere close to convincing her. 'We were, really. What choice did we have? She wanted to go; I couldn't make her stay. Squabbling over how we divided things up wasn't going to change that. I just needed it to be over. To concentrate on getting back on track.'

'And the babies?' Madeleine asked, surprised that Finn was opening up to her. And more than a little intrigued about what exactly it was that Caro had hated so much about her life with Finn. From where Madeleine was sitting, it had quite a lot going for it. And she wasn't thinking about the perfect espresso she'd just downed in two gulps.

'She didn't find out that she was pregnant until quite late on,' Finn said, and once again Madeleine was struck by his honesty. She couldn't believe that he was trusting her with the details of his marriage. Wasn't he worried that she was going to sell him out? 'By then our marriage was already over, and she had accepted a job doing emergency aid work abroad. She wanted the kids raised here, where it was safer. We both did. And she didn't want to turn down a job where she knew she could save thousands of lives.'

So their marriage was already over. That was interesting. She'd assumed that their breakup was a recent thing, with the babies and all, but it sounded as if it must have happened more than a year ago. And all of a sudden, sleeping in his home, with this spark of attraction she was finding hard to ignore, was seeming like a less and less good idea.

'And so now you're a full-time dad,' she stated.

'Well, I'm trying to work as much as I can,' he said with a shrug, that pinched look back around his eyes. 'But at the moment it's just not enough. There's definitely more dadding going on, and I'm grateful for the extra time with them, but I can't let things slide any further with work. I'm hoping that's where you come in, while I find someone more permanent, that is.'

Madeleine nodded, thoughtful. 'I bet people were surprised.'

He frowned for a second before he guessed her meaning. 'That I want to parent my children?' he asked. She saw the hardness appear around his mouth and jaw and heard the sharpness in his tone, and realised that she had hit a nerve. But she hadn't been criticising—either him or Caro. She was just surprised. 'It's just unusual that you're doing it while Caro's abroad,' Madeleine said, pointing out the obvious. 'I didn't mean anything by it.'

'She's a good mum,' Finn said, his face still hard. 'She video calls every day. She comes home when she can. All that she wants is for them to be safe and happy. Thousands of men do the same thing every day and no one bats an eyelid.'

Madeleine sat up straighter, a little indignant that he thought she was judging. 'I wasn't batting! I never questioned that Caro is a good mum. But you can't deny that the situation is unusual, that's all.'

'Look at my life, Madeleine,' Finn said, the muscle in his jaw finally relaxing. 'Everything about it is unusual.'

She nodded. 'It's definitely different from when we were growing up,' she ventured, wondering how he would react to the reminder about his change in circumstances.

'God, I know. If you'd told me then…'

Madeleine smiled, sensing that this was as far as this conversation was going to go.

'So, this pizza, then,' she said, grasping for a change of topic. 'Are these kiddies going to co-operate and let us eat with two hands? Should we wear them out before bedtime?'

'That,' Finn said, standing suddenly, 'is an excellent idea. Let me give you the grand tour, and we can let them have a roll around on their play mat in the nursery while you get settled.'

Madeleine stood and parked Hart on her hip, where he gurgled and babbled as he reached out to Finn and his sister.

'I never knew they were so wriggly at this age,' Madeleine said, pulling Hart in closer so he didn't dive out of her arms.

'You should try it with two of them,' Finn said with a laugh as Bella decided it was her turn to try and escape.

'Just promise you're not going to leave me alone with them just yet,' Madeleine said, her smile fading when she realised that she was basically asking him to spend time with her. That verged dangerously close to needy—and she hated needy.

'I promise, not until you feel you're ready,' Finn said as he led them out of the kitchen and into the hallway, with its elegant sweeping staircase up to the first floor.

'I thought you'd be most comfortable in here,' Finn said, showing her into a guest room. The bed held an imposing number of soft furnishings, but it was the desk in front of the window that caught her eye. An elegant writing desk with a simple Scandinavian aesthetic sat in front of a Juliet balcony looking out on the garden.

Finn must have caught the direction of her interest because he said, 'I had Trudy bring that in here. I wasn't sure if you'd want to write, or if you were working.'

'That is so thoughtful. Thank you.'

'And if there's anything else that you need, just let me know, okay? I want you to feel at home here.'

And, surprisingly, she thought that she might, for the few weeks that she was planning on staying, at least. The luxuries made that easy enough: the sparkling decanter of water on her nightstand, the toiletries that she could glimpse through the open door to her en suite bathroom. It was a far cry from the mould-infested flat that she'd just been evicted from. But it wasn't just the luxury of the place. It just had…a vibe. She wasn't sure what it was. But she felt comfortable here. Maybe it was that she'd known Finn for ever, that he had been a part of her family for as long as she could remember.

But then she looked over at Finn and caught him looking at her. Not at her body—she could tell when men were doing that. But at her. And nothing felt comfortable any more. Because she wasn't sure that she'd ever seen anyone look at her like that. If she'd ever felt a man's eyes on her and not felt as if she was being flayed open and they were peering at her insides.

It was the same reason, she told herself. Finn didn't look at her like that because he'd known her before she had this body. When she'd been a child. Before everyone she met had started judging her on the curves of her breasts and her hips, as if they somehow broadcast something about her personality.

But he *noticed* her body. She'd seen and cringed at enough reactions to her over the years to be able to read a man's mind perfectly when he was looking at her. And Finn's was no different. He saw her curves. He liked them. But she was starting to have the suspicion that he saw beyond them too. That he would still look at her like that whatever shape her body took.

And that was deeply unsettling. Because if there was one thing that she had learnt over the years it was how reliably men reacted to her. What she should expect from them, and what she should ask of them in return. And if she was wrong about that, if Finn was going to tread outside of that familiar, safe territory that she had constructed for herself, then she wasn't sure what to make of it.

She met his eyes and he startled, and that gave her hope. Because, whatever this tension was between them, it seemed as if Finn was as wary of it as she was. And that was good. That meant that they were both going to be on their guard. That they were both going to be committed to keeping these feelings in their place.

She knew why she was so wary. But she wondered about Finn. She had strong suspicions that he was attracted to her. But it was equally clear that he had no intention of acting on that. Why? Was it the divorce? Was he still heartbroken over Caro? She didn't think so. He had sounded a little sad when they had talked about her earlier. But he wasn't yearning for her; she could read that much. But she still wondered what had happened—why they had broken up. They had been together for a couple of years before they had got married, so it wasn't a flash-in-the-pan relationship.

She could ask him, she supposed. But the way that he had shut down her questioning made clear that he didn't want to talk about it, and it wasn't her place to push him. She could ask her brother, but showing that level of interest would open her up to a whole lot of questions from Jake that she had no intention of answering.

Finn showed Madeleine around the apartment, wondering what on earth had made him think that it would be a good idea to spill the details of his marriage and divorce to a journalist. Because, despite their history and their shared childhood memories, Madeleine *was* a journalist. And, more than that, she was a journalist who had recently been made redundant and pitched into an enormously competitive job and freelance market. The woman had to eat, and if she chose to do that by selling the story that he had just willingly spilled to her then who could blame her? He certainly wouldn't.

Back in the day, there was very little

that he wouldn't have done to put food in his belly and a roof over his head. And a decade of more money than he needed had done nothing to dull the memories of those decades of deprivation. And then recently, with his divorce and the developments at work, having to leave the home that he and Caroline had bought together, having to dismantle the life they had created together, he'd found himself staring at his spreadsheets and feeling that familiar nag of worry. An instinct that he'd thought he'd lost years ago.

And Madeleine hadn't forgotten his old life either. He used to turn up at her house with an empty belly, desperately ashamed of the fact that he would willingly raid their fridge for anything that he could get his hands on, and the fact that they all knew the score. They had always tried to cover it up. Looked the other way when their mum had given him the biggest portion at dinner. But they all knew, and he knew that they knew.

The alternative was going hungry, going home to a cold empty house while his mother worked her second job in a futile attempt to make ends meet. And hunger had won out over pride every time. He felt hot at the memories of how low he had had to stoop at that time in his life, and grateful that his children would never ever know that feeling. His mother had done everything that she could for him. She had worked two jobs trying to provide for them, but it had never been enough. Without the Everleigh family, he would have been as lonely as he had been hungry. It was thanks to them that they had all made it through those years. Thanks to them that he had finished his homework and turned up at school.

Now that he was the one with the warm home and the food and the luxury lifestyle, he would never begrudge any of them a single penny. He could never repay what they had given him, no matter how hard he tried. Giving Madeleine his spare room for a few weeks was nothing. Not compared to what she had given him, what she'd shared with him, back when she'd barely acknowledged his existence. She could take it all, as far as he was concerned, for as long as she needed it, and he would still be in her debt.

Getting twin babies to sleep wasn't an easy task at the best of times. When they were overstimulated by a new face and a new playmate who was in no way as immune to their babyish charms as he had had to learn to be, it was damn near impossible. Despite Finn having managed to get two babies into the bathroom at six-thirty, right on schedule, it had been half an hour before they had escaped that steam-filled room with two overtired, giggling, wriggly bundles wrapped in towels. And that had only been the start of the fun and games. It had taken nearly an hour of rocking, bouncing and pacing the hallways to get them both asleep, and in that time he and Madeleine had barely exchanged more than an exasperated glance as they'd passed one another in the hallway.

He had seen the shock starting to fade and the reality of what she had let herself in for starting to sink in as the babies had fought sleep, or being put down in their cots, over and over. And over. By the time that they'd both slowly backed out of the nursery, breath held and the door gently closed, he was ready to sink into bed and call it a night. But Madeleine was his guest and he knew that Jake expected more of him than to leave her to fend for herself the first night she was here.

That was all it was, he told himself. He owed it to Jake to make sure that Madeleine was settled and happy and had everything she needed. There was no other reason that the idea of sharing a pizza with her had sustained him all evening. It would be absolutely inappropriate for him to think of her as anything other than Jake's sister and his temporary saviour. It absolutely was not—in any way—a date.

So why did he feel so nervous?

He didn't even get nervous before dates. At least he didn't think that he did. Since he and Caro had decided that their marriage was over, he hadn't been on one. Until the twins were a couple of months old he had seen Caro almost as much as when they were married—just because he was no longer her husband didn't mean that he wasn't going to support her through the pregnancy and take care of her afterwards, until she was ready to take up her new job. But, all that aside, what would be the point in dating when he knew that he would never have a serious relationship again? The last—as amicably as it had ended—had threatened everything that he had worked for over the last decade. Had seen him taking on financial uncertainty that he still wasn't sure that he was going to survive. He was never going through that again. He just couldn't take the risk.

Until he had opened the door to Madeleine Everleigh, and his decision to stay permanently single didn't seem quite so simple.

Which left his love life…where? In the realm of hook-ups and one-night stands and casual flings? And when it came to Madeleine…he couldn't think of a less appropriate relationship to have with his best friend's sister. Jake had been best man at his wedding. He couldn't even think about a casual hook-up with the man's sister. Except…he was thinking about it.

Oh, was he thinking about it.

And it wasn't even Madeleine's body he was thinking about. It was her eyes that he couldn't get out of his mind. The way that she looked at him and saw the smooth businessman and the frazzled dad and the scared kid all at once. They weren't separate people to her, the way that they were to everyone else in his life. The circles of his business life and his childhood friends and his social life never crossed. He squeezed himself into those different personas as he put on his suit for work or clipped himself into a baby carrier and headed to a playgroup. But not with Madeleine.

He'd never felt the strangeness of that with Jake. Maybe because he had never looked at Jake and had the instant flash of desire he had with Madeleine. With Madeleine? It was hard to think about anything else. Especially now she was here in his home, settling in with her things, playing with his kids and drinking his coffee. Merging their lives for the next few weeks.

Even with Caro there had been barriers between the different parts of his life. She had accompanied him to work functions. Slipped smoothly through the networking and the business dinners that were expected of her. But she had never slipped so comfortably into his past, the parts of his life that were harder to face. She'd never been comfortable with his mother. He could never have taken her to see the tiny flat where he had grown up.

Absurd, really, given that she was dedicating her life to ending child poverty. She wouldn't have judged him. But he didn't want to be a project to her. He didn't want to be one of the kids she was rescuing.

With Madeleine, nothing had to be said. Or hidden. Or tiptoed around. She knew it all. She knew how bad it had been, and how high he had risen, and she saw that he was the same person wherever he was living. And the thought of that, of the two parts of his life being reconciled, was troubling. And intoxicating.

He showed Madeleine back down to the kitchen and hunted out the pizza menus he kept in a drawer for weekends when he couldn't be bothered to cook. It wouldn't be long now before the babies were eating real food and he would actually have to produce something that they could all eat together, rather than just steaming them some carrot sticks. But for a few more weeks, at least, his weekends could be eighty per cent pepperoni. He handed Madeleine a menu and headed to the fridge to find them both a beer.

'We can take the drinks out on the balcony if you like,' Finn suggested, glancing over at Madeleine. 'There's a nice view of the park.'

'Sure,' she replied with a shrug, eyes still on the menu. 'Sounds like a plan. I'll bring my phone and we can order from there.'

CHAPTER FOUR

MADELEINE FOLLOWED FINN up the stairs, still trying to keep her mind on the pizza menu in order to stop it wandering anywhere more dangerous than that. Like up a couple of steps to where Finn's behind was almost exactly at her eye line, and way, *way* too tempting to look at. He might have been a skinny kid when she'd first known him, but he wasn't any longer. He'd shown her the gym in the basement of the apartment building, and it seemed he made good use of it. She knew that if she let her gaze wander up over the edge of the menu she would see strong, thick thighs and a perfect firm backside.

All that from sneaking glances, then stopping herself as soon as she realised what she was doing. And it had been enough all day to keep her cheeks colouring, and illicit thoughts in her brain. She thought that she might combust if she actually allowed herself to get a proper eyeful.

Finn turned right at the top of the stairs, taking her down a corridor they hadn't covered in their tour earlier. And when he pushed open a door it took her a few moments to realise what she was looking at.

The duvet had been hastily pulled back on the bed, a phone was charging on the bedside table beside a creased paperback and half-empty glass of water. A pile of clothes had been discarded on the way to the bathroom, the door to which stood ajar on the far wall.

She took a step back, her heart caught in her throat as she tried to process this information. She'd thought they were going out onto the balcony for a drink. But instead he had brought her here, to what was unmistakably his bedroom. Was this a trick? She took another step back, her heart pounding in her chest as she tried to assess her options. She could just head for the front door. Run out and not look back. She could back away slowly, and hope that he didn't turn nasty when he didn't get what he wanted.

How many years had she been making these calculations—trying to find a way out of trouble when her body gave men ideas that she had no intention of going along with? Somehow, somewhere along the line, it had become her job to let them down gently. To avoid the nasty consequences she knew could follow if she didn't handle their fragile little egos carefully enough as she rejected their advances.

How had she really misread the situation here so badly? she asked herself. Sure, she had sensed that spark of interest from Finn. She guessed that he liked her body. But somehow she hadn't sensed danger here. Was that because she had been attracted to him too? Had that put her off her guard, led her into this dangerous situation? She tried to think again whether she had said something or done something to make him think that this was what she wanted.

Because this wasn't what she wanted. Just because she might have fantasised about more at some point, that didn't mean that that was where she was at right now. She wasn't so stupid to think that she could just have desires and act on them.

She heard a weird gargle form in her throat and had just about made up her mind to run when Finn turned and looked at her. She saw the expression in his eyes change from confusion to shock when he took in her expression. She gripped a little tighter to her phone, just in case she had to use it, and inched back when Finn squared up to her.

'Madeleine…' He spoke slowly, as if to a spooked animal, and she wondered what was showing on her face to make him think he needed to.

'This is your bedroom,' Madeleine spat out, taking control of the situation. 'You didn't say anything about your bedroom,' she went on, making sure he knew that she wasn't going to be swept along with something. That she knew what she wanted and didn't want right now and was going to stand up for herself.

'I'm so sorry,' Finn said, holding his hands up, still using that slow calm tone that made her think she had rabbit-in-the-headlights eyes. 'I should have explained we need to get to the balcony through my bedroom. Out there,' he said, gesturing towards the French windows, covered with gauzy voile curtains. 'The lock is stuck on the other door out and at the moment this is the only way. I'm sorry I didn't explain that before we came up here.'

He looked at her for a moment longer, and she wondered what he was seeing. She was frozen in the doorway, her hand locked tight around her phone, her mind stuck in another moment of fight or flight. Another time where she had thought she was safe, only to be blindsided with a man's demands on her. She had run then, and it had destroyed her career before it had even begun. It had led her to the mouldy little bedsit she had been existing in until she had been evicted and found herself on Finn's doorstep.

So what should she do now? Fight? This was the only source of income, the only roof over her head, that she had for the foreseeable future, until she figured out what she was going to do with the rest of her life. Flight? She could run, to Jake's. He would make room for her, no matter how cramped it left his family. But she hadn't wanted to impose before and still didn't now. And he was Finn's best friend. What if he asked why she had left? *If?* Of course he would ask, and she didn't know what she would tell him.

Finn took a step towards her and she took another two back, glancing over her shoulder just for a fraction of a second to judge the distance to the stairs before looking back at Finn, making sure she had re-established the space between them. He shut the bedroom door firmly and leaned back against it, crossing his arms over his body, creating a barrier between them. His face was hard and tough, and she wasn't sure whether the suppressed anger she saw there was directed at her. There wasn't anyone else here.

'Madeleine, I'm so sorry that I scared you,' he said. 'That was thoughtless of me. I promise you have nothing to be afraid of. I didn't mean anything by bringing you to my bedroom, other than a way to get out onto the balcony.'

'I wasn't scared,' she bit out automatically. She could lie to him, but she couldn't lie to herself. Her mouth still carried the bitter tang of blood where she had bitten the inside of her cheek and she could still hear the pounding of her blood as it raced around her body, bringing oxygen to the big muscles of her limbs, readying her for battle.

She hesitated for a moment, let her blood pressure drop a fraction, and then a fraction more, Finn still standing dead still against the door to his bedroom. She looked behind her again, making sure she had space to run if she needed it.

'If you want to leave, I'll get you a car right away,' he said. 'It can take you to Jake's. Or a hotel. Wherever you would feel safe.'

'I can order my own ride,' she said on reflex, before she had really had a chance to process his words. He was offering her a way out. He was giving her sanctuary. Why would he do that if he was a threat to her? She looked up and met his eyes for the first time since they had left the kitchen, and the compassion she read there almost broke her. The adrenaline left her body in a rush, leaving her limp and soft, and she slumped back against the wall. Finn wasn't a threat. This apartment was safe. She was safe. He was the boy that she had known most of her life, and he wanted to protect her.

'I'm sorry,' she said, letting her head drop back against the wall and trying to slow her heart rate.

'Don't apologise,' he ordered, looking her hard in the eye. 'Are you okay?'

'Getting there,' Madeleine admitted, letting her eyes shut, blocking out the world for just a minute.

'Do you want to talk about it?' Finn asked, his voice as soft as she had ever heard it. She was tempted, for a moment. For no reason other than to explain what must have looked like truly bizarre behaviour. But she had carried this secret for more years than she cared to think about. And she had always believed that it was best that way. What was done was done, and talking about it wasn't going to change anything. More than that, talking about it was going to slice into a well-healed wound and make her bleed again, and she had absolutely no desire to give that a try.

Except…except how well healed could it be, really, when this was her reaction to something so minor? She had completely overreacted to an innocent move on Finn's part. Perhaps reopening that wound would be necessary, one of these days, and looking a little closer at what had got her blood pumping just then.

But she couldn't do it now. Not when her body was winding down from that burst of panic and her limbs felt like noodles. Not when Finn's eyes were on her, seeing more than she'd ever intended to show him.

'Pizza,' she said at last, loosening her grip on her phone and the sweaty flyer now scrunched in her palm.

Finn raised his eyes, assessing this change in the subject, whether he was going to push her more or let the matter drop. To her relief, he unfolded his arms and nodded.

'You order. I'm going to check on the kids and I'll meet you in the kitchen in a bit.'

Space. Silence. Thank God.

She walked down the stairs and perched on a stool in the kitchen, concentrating her whole mind on the simple task of ordering pizza. Because, if she let it wander, all she could see was Finn's face as she'd stood in front of him, looking at him as if he was a sexual predator, her body primed to fight him. She didn't want to think about what he was thinking right now. She couldn't afford to wonder what was going through his mind as he peeked in on the babies and made sure that they were sleeping soundly.

Maybe she should just go, be a burden on her brother for a few weeks. Sleep on her nephews' bedroom floor amidst the discarded Lego and Pokémon cards.

Or she could leave London. Go travelling. What, with all the money that she had stashed away for a rainy day from her subsistence-level wage from a second-rate gossip site? Maybe she could find a job at a local paper somewhere dull and anonymous and spend the rest of her life chasing stories about lost kittens and parish council in-fighting. Any of those options looked preferable to having to face Finn when he came back downstairs.

The buzz from the front door intercom interrupted her thoughts. Pizza. Whatever decisions she had to make, she would make them with a full stomach, even if that did mean facing Finn. She wasn't stupid enough to launch herself out into the night hungry.

As she brought the pizzas back through to the kitchen she heard Finn's footsteps behind her and felt the colour rising in her cheeks before she'd even turned around to look at him.

'Hey,' he said, his voice hesitant as she opened up the cardboard boxes and they were hit by the smell of melted cheese and crisp dough.

'Hey.' She forced a smile and hoped that it looked less creaky than it felt. She leaned back on the breakfast bar to eat. Last time they had tried to find an alternative venue it had gone so horribly wrong. And she felt secure with that huge chunk of granite between them. Not that she thought that she had anything to fear from Finn any more. It was just that she thought if he got any closer she might actually melt from shame, if the floor wasn't kind enough to simply swallow her whole before that could happen.

'Look, about what happened—' Finn started, but she jumped in before he could finish.

'Really, you don't have to… I'm sorry I overreacted. It's nothing.'

'It's not nothing, Madeleine. You're my guest and I need to know that you feel safe here. I'm going to say this now so it's out there. I know that there's some sort of chemistry between us—I feel it, and I think you do too. But here's the thing—I'm not going to do anything about it. You have absolutely nothing to worry about on that front. I wasn't trying to get you into bed, and I'm not going to. You're Jake's sister, practically family, and I would never risk that over something… I just don't want you to think that that's what I had in mind when I invited you here,' he went on. 'I don't want you thinking you have to be on your guard around me. You're safe here.'

It was what she wanted to hear. She was safe. She was protected. She hadn't wanted him to be trying to engineer her into bed.

And yet…it still felt brutal, somehow. The way that he said it—he was never going to do anything about it. The absolute certainty in his voice when he told her that he wasn't interested in her.

Well, that was fine because she'd had

every intention of shutting her own feelings down. This would only make that easier. She could carry on with her role as nanny, or babysitter, or best friend's sister, or whatever she was to him, without any added complications.

Fine.

She was absolutely fine with that.

CHAPTER FIVE

TORTURE. THAT WAS the only word that could adequately describe the past hour. First, that look in Madeleine's eyes when she'd thought that he was trying to trick her. Now this, having to tell her that he had absolutely no interest in following through on his feelings for her, because it was suddenly clear to him that this chemistry between them wasn't important. What was important was protecting Madeleine, and his place in her life—as part of her family. And that meant never following where that spark between them might lead.

There was no hiding the look in her eyes when they had been on the landing upstairs. She had been terrified. Looking for the exits, calculating risks. So sure that she was in danger. He couldn't believe that he had been so stupid. That it hadn't occurred to him to mention that the only way out onto the balcony was through his bedroom.

But there was more to the story too. He was sure of that. The look in her eyes and that reaction—they didn't come from no-where. And that meant that someone in her past had hurt her. He had been surprised by the rage he had felt when he had realised that. The overwhelming desire to hunt down the person that had made Madeleine so afraid, and to make sure that he could never get to her again. But there was no way that he could say that to Madeleine. Because the minute that he had suggested that she might want to talk about it, her shutters had come down. She'd looked as terrified at the pros-pect of that as she had at the thought of him trying to trap her in his bedroom.

So he'd done the only thing he could think to do—he'd said what he had to, to make her feel safe. He'd decided that that was more important than any hopes he might have had that this chemistry might lead somewhere. Because of course he had been interested. In other circumstances. If things had been different. If his business had been more stable. If his divorce hadn't left him convinced that he needed to stay single to protect the life that he had built for himself, then he would *definitely* have been interested. But now that he had seen she was scared of him? None of that mattered anyway. He never wanted to see that look in her eyes again.

So now he wasn't interested, he told himself. It wasn't a lie. Because it didn't matter what chemical reaction his body threw up when he looked at her, he was more than just an animal reacting to his hormones or his basest desires. He was an adult with full control over himself. And he was using that control now to shut down any hint of attraction towards her. His only priority now was making sure that she felt safe. That nothing could hurt her while she was under his roof.

Thank God she had turned down his offer to get her a car. Because he had never felt such a strong urge to protect someone before. If he'd had to send her out into the night with no idea where she was going, he didn't think he could have borne it.

He hoped she felt safe now.

He risked a look at her over his pizza

slice, and found her eyes on him. As their gazes met he hesitated, wanting again to ask her what had happened to provoke such a strong reaction. Wanting to ask how he could fix it. And then remembering that it wasn't his place to ask. She didn't want to share what had happened with him, and he had no right to push. He had no right to anything. She was Jake's sister, and that made her feel like family to him, but he had no expectation that she returned the feeling. To her he was probably just the annoying little kid at the end of her dining table, talking Lego and Nintendo with her brother. He was constantly surprised that she remembered him at all.

The fact that Jake thought of him like a brother didn't automatically extend that feeling to Madeleine. They had barely spoken when they were kids. The two-year difference in age had been a gulf that had stretched too far between them. Separating their lives into different worlds. She might as well have been an alien for all they had had in common when she was fourteen and he was twelve.

'Good pizza,' she said at last, when the

silence had stretched out to unbearable. He looked away as she broke their gaze and started to lick the grease from her fingers. Principled he might be, but he wasn't a saint.

'Yeah, I'm a good customer,' he replied, trying to keep his mind on the food. He glanced up at the clock. It was still early, really early. But he had the perfect excuse to hide away from her tonight.

'Look, I'm sorry to leave you to your own devices your first night here, but would you mind if I turned in? The twins still have a midnight feed, and I could grab an hour or two of sleep before I have to do that.'

'Of course,' she said, looking relieved. 'Will you need my help—?'

'No,' he jumped in. The last thing that they both needed was an impromptu meeting in the middle of the night. 'It's fine. I can handle it. You need anything before I go up?'

She shook her head, and for a second he thought that she was going to say something more. But then she dropped her head and he knew the moment had passed.

'Goodnight,' he said, then turned for the door without waiting for a reply.

CHAPTER SIX

THE NEXT MORNING Madeleine fought the arrival of the sunlight around the edges of the curtains in her room and wished that she'd had the foresight to close the shutters before she'd come to bed last night. With how discombobulated she'd been feeling, it was really a wonder that she'd managed to pull on some pyjamas and wipe off her make-up, never mind fiddling with the pristinely restored period features of the building.

How long could she get away with hiding up here? she wondered. She was under no illusions that the reason for Finn's ridiculously early night last night was because the atmosphere had gone from awkward to worse. All because of her stupid overreaction to seeing the inside of Finn's bedroom.

A large part of her insides wanted to curl up and die this morning, when she remembered how she had reacted. The pumping blood. The wild eyes. The implicit accusation in her response.

Not implicit. Explicit. So explicit, in fact, that Finn had felt it necessary to tell her in the baldest possible way that he was not interested in having sex with her. She blushed again at the memory. She was meant to be his guest. But her hair-trigger reaction to the smallest of misunderstandings had meant she'd all but accused him of planning to try and molest her.

No wonder he had chosen to spend the rest of the evening away from her.

She wished that she could check out of her brain sometimes too. Leave the flashbacks and the panic aside, and just live like a normal person. React in a totally normal way to totally normal stimuli.

The sound of a baby crying reached up to her first-floor room and when the second baby joined in she knew that she had to move. She was meant to be helping out with the kids and hiding up here wasn't just childish, it was dereliction of duty. A duty that just happened to be keeping a roof over her head and her bank balance in the black.

She pulled a big soft wrap cardigan on over her jersey pants and sleep top, and pulled her hair back into a reasonably respectable ponytail. Drawing back the curtains, she realised she'd been missing out on a truly glorious day. The park in the middle of the square was bathed in golden sunshine and the sky was a deep clear blue. It was enough to blow the cobwebs off her bad mood and actually make her smile.

When she reached the kitchen, Finn was bouncing Bella on his shoulder while making up a bottle, and both babies seemed to be competing to see which could make the most ear-splitting noise. Hart, in a bouncy seat on the floor, looked—or sounded—to be winning, so she scooped him up, taking a moment to fuss over him before turning to Finn. She held her breath for a moment, not sure whether things would be weird this morning, and praying that he had scrubbed the previous evening from his memory.

'Oh, thank God you're here,' he said with a smile, hitching Bella higher on his shoulder as he scooped formula into little plastic pots. 'They don't usually gang up on me like this, but when they do—boy, do they go for it. Here, do you think you can manage Bella too?'

Before she had a chance to say no, she had a baby parked on each hip while Finn screwed lids onto bottles and wiped down countertops.

'I was thinking we should go out for the day,' Finn said. 'Enjoy the sunshine. There's only so much you can do to entertain these two indoors.'

'Sounds great. What did you have in mind?' she asked, grateful that they weren't going to spend the day inside. It didn't matter how luxurious the surroundings were. If the atmosphere was as tense as it had been the previous evening, then it would be completely unbearable.

'Well, I've never taken them to the beach,' Finn said, putting away the tin of formula. 'It's too nice a day to spend half of it in traffic getting to the coast, but there's a pop-up beach I read about that might be fun. It might also be a nightmare of sand-encrusted toddlers. But worth a try?'

'Definitely worth a try,' Madeleine said, marvelling that the twins were both quieting down as she bounced them gently. 'Do

I even want to know what packing a bag for twins at the beach looks like?' she asked with a dubious look at the backpack slung over the back of one of the dining chairs.

'It's terrifying,' Finn confirmed with a laugh. 'But I'll talk you through it. And there should be enough stuff in the fridge to pack a decent picnic. Trudy has a habit of predicting my impulses on such a regular basis it makes me wonder how impulsive I really am.'

'Did you know that the best indicator of the number of barbecues on a Saturday is the temperature on the preceding Tuesday? Sounds like Trudy has a good grip on economics,' Madeleine said. 'Right, give me a list of what the kids need and I'll go find it in their room. Then we can raid the fridge together. Sound like a plan?'

'Great,' Finn said, before reeling off a list of clothing and supplies that Madeleine was sure could outfit a military unit for several weeks. But as she packed tiny clothes into an enormous bag she was glad of the practical challenges that a day out with the babies would pose. She wanted her time filled—every second of it, if possible—because the alternative was awkward silences or, worse, awkward conversation.

By the time that she got downstairs, Bella and Hart were in their car seats and Finn was looking at his phone. 'The car's outside whenever we're ready,' he said, looking up at her with a smile. 'Did you find everything?'

'I think so. I mean, how badly can it go?'

'Well, I've been out with them before and they've pooed through every item of clothing in the bag and I've run out of wipes halfway through the day. But sure, nothing worse than that.'

'We're going into central London. They have baby wipes there. We'll be fine,' she said with a confidence that she didn't feel.

'I'll hold you to that,' Finn said with a laugh, sliding his phone in his pocket and reaching for one of the car seats. 'Do you mind grabbing Hart? I cannot tell you what a luxury it is not to have to lug all this stuff on my own.'

'Sure. That's what I'm here for,' Madeleine said, and was grateful for the little reminder to herself. She was only here to look after the children. Last night had been awkward, but they just had to ignore it. It wasn't as if they even had a friendship that they had to rescue. Just because he was friends with Jake didn't mean he was her friend too. All they had to think about was the children—and she could do that.

Just from the half day she had spent with them already, she knew that they were more than capable of filling her time and her thoughts. But their dad did keep trying to muscle in there too. No, that wasn't fair. That made it sound like Finn's fault, and it wasn't. It was entirely her fault that she couldn't stop thinking about him. It had been bad enough, even before that incident on the landing last night. But this morning it was worse.

Because yesterday—it was a fun little fantasy. Something that she knew that she was never going to act on. Something that she knew couldn't hurt her. But today... today was different.

Because once Finn had mentioned his attraction—the chemistry between them—it had breached an unspoken rule where they were just refusing to acknowledge that it existed. And even though Finn had said that he wasn't interested in acting on their feelings, she wasn't sure that she believed him. It had felt brutal last night, when he had said the words.

But this morning she could see the bigger picture. She knew that there had been a spark there when she had arrived. And she knew what a fright she must have looked when she had freaked out about his bedroom. She didn't want him to be attracted to her. God knew she didn't want to be attracted to him. If they could go along with what he had said and just try and ignore these feelings, that would make life so much easier for the next few weeks.

As the car sat and idled in the London traffic she busied herself with fussing over the babies, glad that the four-by-four had enough space that she wasn't pressed against Finn's thigh. She wasn't sure how long she'd be able to kid herself that she had absolutely no feelings about him if she had the firm press of his muscle against her skin.

Up in her room, she had agonised over what to wear. A visit to the beach didn't usually see her at her most comfortable at the best of times, but she suspected that a visit to the beach with Finn by her side would make her more self-conscious still. The fact that the beach happened to be in the middle of London, the largest and most densely populated city in the country, was actually a godsend. There would be no room for relaxed, reclined sunbathing. She thought that they would be lucky to find somewhere to plonk the babies down on the sand, never mind find a space for them to sit.

And if there was no sunbathing there was absolutely no need for a swimsuit. She'd pulled on cropped culottes, a tank top and Wayfarer shades, sure that she would be grateful for the dark lenses to hide behind later in the day.

She couldn't shake those words from her head. He was attracted to her. Why did that bother her so much? No, that was the wrong question. She knew why she was so bothered by them. It was because she felt the same. Having that information out in the open was meant to defuse the situation, but it didn't feel like that right now. Once the shock of last night's encounter had worn off, the knowledge that their attraction was mutual had left an electric fizz in the air.

Not that it mattered any more, because after what had happened there was no way that he would be interested in her. Attraction—liking her body and her face—was one thing. Being willing to take on her trunkful of emotional baggage was quite another. And it was clear from the look on his face last night—even without him stating it as clearly as he had—that he absolutely wasn't interested.

And who could blame him?

Finally the car pulled up near to the pop-up beach, and she made herself busy fishing bags and sunshades and stray baby hats out of the boot of the car while Finn flipped out the pushchair with practised ease and started buckling Hart into one side. She fetched Bella from her car seat, stowed bags underneath and then took a step back to marvel at the sheer amount of stuff that they had brought with them.

'I am never ever doing this on my own,' she stated, only half joking. 'Can I be one of those completely useless nannies that you have to take time off work to supervise because you're worried they might leave the babies behind somewhere?'

Finn shrugged, all mock-casual in a way that had her softening towards him when she'd been so *so* sure that she could resist that charm of his. 'Only if you don't mind me telling Jake how useless you are.'

She laughed, her body instantly relaxing into it, despite her better judgement. 'You know it's really not fair to keep bringing him up like that,' she said, swatting at him good-humouredly as they clipped the babies into their pram seats. 'Pulling out sibling rivalry is below the belt. We left school behind more than a decade ago. We should really act like it.'

'I'm only joking with you because you know you will be completely fine. By the end of the weekend you're going to have the little ones wrapped around your little finger. You'll be making up a bottle with one hand and drinking a cup of tea with the other and rocking the crib with your foot.'

'Ha. I'm glad you have such faith in me.' She couldn't help but feel a little glow that his confidence in her was genuine. She knew that he wouldn't take risks with his kids and if he said that he trusted her she knew that he meant it.

They walked along the river, Madeleine enjoying the feel of the sun warming the top of her head. She could hear the beach before she could see it, the squeals of excited children building the closer they came.

'I'm starting to think this might not have been my best idea,' Finn said after a particularly piercing shriek.

'Ah, come on, it'll be fine,' Madeleine said, nudging him with her shoulder. 'And if it's not, there are plenty of places to escape to.' When they reached the beach— really just a huge sandpit—it wasn't as busy as Madeleine had feared. The summer holiday rush still hadn't hit, she figured, and there were just a few boisterous pre-schoolers making most of the noise.

She shook out the picnic blanket while Finn tackled the straps on the pushchair, and soon they had Bella and Hart rolling on the blanket between them, while Madeleine kicked off her sandals and leaned back on the changing bag as a makeshift beach pillow.

'This was most definitely an excellent idea,' she said, feeling herself sinking a little heavier into the sand, heat coming up through the blanket and the sunlight filtering down through the leaves of a nearby tree. The babies were contentedly gurgling as they lay on the blanket and the pre-schoolers had made a hasty exit when she had subtly mentioned that there were fountains to be run through nearby.

'I'm not going to argue with you. Good ideas are one of my many charms,' Finn said, his voice treacly and relaxed as hers. She didn't need to open her eyes and look over at him to know that he had adopted a similar position to her, stretched out on the sand.

Hart rolled over onto his tummy, nudging at her thigh with a fist, and she opened her eyes with a smile, her heart melting a fraction when she saw him grinning up at her with excitement in his eyes.

'Have they played in the sand before?' she asked Finn, rolling onto her side so that she could tickle Hart, and soaking in the sound of his gorgeous baby gurgle. Really, these kids were impossibly cute. No wonder Finn wanted to spend as much time with them as possible. If they were her kids, she wasn't sure that she would be able to tear herself away from them either.

'Nope. First time,' Finn said, cracking an eye open and smiling at the sight of Hart on his tummy.

'If only he would learn to roll back,' he said. 'In five minutes he'll be bored and annoyed that he's stuck like that.'

'Better give him something to do then,' Madeleine said, scooching him round so that he was at the edge of the blanket. Hart reached out into the warm sand, but then drew his hand back quickly in shock.

Finn laughed, and Madeleine couldn't help but join in. 'Maybe he needs backup,' Finn said, moving Bella so that she could touch the sand too. She reached out but, unlike her brother, buried her hand and giggled as she found the cooler damp sand under the top layer.

'I guess we know who the thrill-seeker is,' Madeleine said. 'Are they always like that?'

'Hart's definitely more sensitive,' Finn said with a smile. 'He's braver when Bella's around. It's one of the more adorable things about them.'

'Are there less adorable things about them?'

'I'll let you ask me that at three tomorrow morning. Hey, kidding,' he added, and she wondered what had shown on her face. 'You don't have to get up in the night with them.'

'No, I'm here to help,' she said, drawing her eyebrows together and wondering why he was looking so warily at her. 'I'm happy to do it. That's the whole point of me coming to stay.'

'But...' He hesitated, and Madeleine knew from the look on his face that he was thinking about what had happened the night before. It wasn't going away, she realised. They had spent the last hour or two pretending that nothing out of the ordinary had happened, but it had been there the whole time, hovering over them, adding pressure to their day.

'Go on,' Madeleine said, aware that they were opening a can of worms. 'Say what you were going to say.'

'It's just… I wouldn't expect you to do the night shift on your own. And I'm worried that if we were to see each other like that—upstairs, in the middle of the night—that it would make you…uncomfortable. And that is the last thing I want.'

She sat up, drawing her knees up to her chest, and tried to fix him with a solid, stern look. 'You don't have to tiptoe around me, Finn. I'm not going to swoon or faint or have a panic attack if I see you after ten p.m. I'm really not the swooning type.'

'I never said you were,' Finn said, mirroring her body language and sitting upright beside her. 'But something happened last night, and I don't want to make you feel that way again.'

'You won't,' she promised, hoping that her voice sounded as sure as she felt. 'It wasn't you who made me feel like that anyway. It was me, being irrational.'

'I don't know about irrational.' Finn's face softened. 'Seemed like you were in a place where rational or irrational didn't mean much. You just looked frightened. And you don't have to tell me why, if you don't want. But you can't stop me wanting to do everything in my power to stop you ever feeling like that again.'

She shook her head. 'That's not your job.'

'I never said it was a job. But you're… we're… You're my friend, Madeleine, and I don't want to see my friend hurting like that.'

'We're not friends, Finn,' she said softly, meeting his gaze. 'We've never been friends.'

She didn't say it to hurt him, and she didn't expect the expression on his face— as if she'd struck him.

'I'm sorry,' she added quickly. 'I didn't mean it as a bad thing. It's just…true. We aren't, really. Are we? We've never hung out. You don't call or text for a chat. And that's fine. You're Jake's friend, and you're a part of the family. But I don't think we're friends.'

He stared at her for a long time, and she wished she could crack open that skull and see what he was thinking. What the narrowing of his eyes and the crease of his brow meant.

'I'd like to be,' he said at last. 'If we're

living together, however temporarily, it would be nice if we were friends.'

She sighed. 'You're just saying this because I freaked out last night. You don't have to do this. I'm not some fragile little girl who needs looking after.'

He actually laughed at that. '*Fragile?* You think I think you're fragile? Last night I thought you might punch me. Or kick me in the balls… I never thought for a second you were fragile. Angry, yes. Frightened, yes. But never fragile.'

'Really? I looked like that to you?' She couldn't help smiling at the thought of that. Because she hadn't felt it. Hadn't felt strong. But it turned out she quite liked knowing how Finn saw her. She had felt cornered and vulnerable. But it turned out her reaction to those feelings had been very much in the fight camp, and she gave herself a little mental pat on the back for that. Once upon a time, she'd frozen. And then run. She wished that in the past she'd had that anger, that fire she had now. She could have directed it at the person who'd really deserved it rather than an innocent bystander.

'I… It wasn't you I was mad at.'

'I guessed as much,' Finn said, dipping his head to meet her gaze when she tried to look away. She followed it back up, determined to be the fighter that he had said he'd seen in her, rather than meekly dropping her head as if she'd been the one in the wrong.

'Do you want to talk about it?' he asked. And she didn't. She never had. But…she couldn't bear the tiptoeing. Couldn't bear the fact that she'd come to stay to help him out with the kids and now he thought that she couldn't handle the night shift in case she bumped into him in the dark.

But talking about last night… That was complicated. Because it wasn't just how she had acted. It was what he had said. He had just come straight out with it. He was attracted to her. He acknowledged the spark and the chemistry between them as if it was the most normal thing in the world. But it didn't feel normal to her to be having that conversation. What was she meant to say—yes, you were right, I'm totally hot for you and desperately trying to ignore it because doing anything else would be a spectacularly bad idea? That didn't sound like a fun conversation. That sounded awkward and painful and suited to somewhere other than a kids' sandpit.

And if they acknowledged those feelings here in the daylight, out in the real world, then how were they meant to carry on as normal? Sure, he had mentioned it last night. But those were extenuating circumstances. He had said it because she was having a major freak-out and he needed to clear the air for her to feel safe. That didn't mean that he wanted to talk about it again, that he thought that those feelings meant anything—that they were important in any way.

They weren't important to her. How could they be? So, he was attracted to her. Big deal: a lot of guys were. Since she'd been a teenager, her life had been a string of guys making a big deal out of how attracted to her they were, whether she was interested in their attention or not. Usually not.

But not this time.

And when she thought back to what he had said, he hadn't actually said that he was attracted to her. Hadn't mentioned her boobs or her body, like half the guys who came onto her, thinking that that was what she would want to hear. No, he had talked about connection. About spark. About something mutual between them. And that was dangerous. She wasn't worried that he thought she was attractive. She was worried about the fact that he could see her attraction to him. That she wasn't imagining the spark of something between them.

How long had it been there? She couldn't be sure. It wasn't there the first time they'd met, when he was a skinny, scrawny eleven-year-old and she was a sullen thirteen. Had it been there at Jake's wedding five years ago? Thank goodness Jake and his husband had passed on the big traditional do and had listened to her insistence that she didn't need to be a bridesmaid. For a fleeting second she felt the horror of being matched with Finn as the best man. Except Caro had been there anyway, smiling at Finn's side for the best part of the day. Madeleine had given them a wide berth and had made polite conversation with Finn only when necessary.

No, she and Finn had never been friends, but now she found herself asking why that was. Why had there always been that distance between them, which had only seemed to get wider when he had married Caro?

Had she known on some level that these feelings had been growing under the surface all along? Had he? After all, he was the one who had called them out into the open now. Was it so difficult to imagine that he had been aware of them before this week?

Had she been aware of them? Never consciously. She was sure of that.

She had held Finn at arm's length for as long as she had known him, as she had every other man in her life. Even those who had made it into her bed were still considered with a healthy amount of suspicion— if all they were interested in was her body then what was the point of letting them closer? Had she done the same with Finn— what, out of habit? And missed the fact that he seemed to be an actual good guy?

'I don't want to go into details,' she said, shuddering at the thought, and wondering how to tell the story in as few words as possible. Writing tight copy was her speciality. This should be as easy as breathing for her. But when her life was the story it didn't seem so simple. 'I got stuck in a room where I didn't want to be. With someone I didn't want to be there with. I got out, but not entirely unscathed, I think we can say after last night. I'm sorry that I tarred you with the same brush. I didn't mean to imply anything. It just triggered me, I guess, and I wasn't thinking rationally after that.'

She watched as his jaw tensed, then his eyes softened. 'I'm so sorry that that happened.' His voice was gruff, and she wished she knew him well enough to understand the emotion she heard in it. 'Is there anything else I can do to make you feel safe?' he asked.

Madeleine shook her head, wishing she could go back in time to a point where Finn didn't think that it was his responsibility to take care of her.

'I do feel safe,' she told him. 'I'm sorry that I made you think that I don't.'

'You have nothing to apologise for. I

don't want you to ever feel like you have to say sorry for that.'

'I freaked out.' She sat up a little straighter, the memory of the previous evening making it impossible for her to relax. 'I basically accused you of…'

'You didn't.' He reached out a hand to cover hers and she started at the feel of his skin on hers. She had to force herself to remain still. Not to react how she wanted, to turn her palm over. To slide her fingers between his and hold on. 'You reacted to a situation instinctively to protect yourself.' He went on, 'Never apologise for that.'

'Well…thanks.' She pulled her hand away, breathing a sigh of relief at the clarity it brought. Trying not to think too hard about why such a simple touch made thinking so difficult. 'I feel like you're being much nicer about this than I deserve.'

'Why wouldn't you deserve me being nice to you, Madeleine?'

She stopped short at his words. No one had done this before. No one had made her stop and think about why she said certain things. Why she thought about her past in a certain way. But now Finn was holding up a mirror to how she had acted last night and, instead of looking away, she wanted to see more. Wanted to understand why she had made the decisions that she had. She'd been hiding from her past for more years than she cared to admit.

But it wasn't his job to tease that out with her. He had done enough by making her think of that time, that maybe it was time to reopen that wound and see if there was anything that could be done about making it heal a little smoother this time.

'I… I don't have an answer for that today,' she replied at last, realising that she had left him hanging. 'But I'm grateful to have you,' she added, meaning it. Whatever weird feelings she was having for him, she was thankful that she had freaked out on someone so obstinately determined to be supportive. 'Do we need to talk about what you said? About…chemistry? If you're going to find it awkward, me being here, maybe I should think about finding some-where else to stay.'

'We can talk about it if you want. If you feel we need to. I'm sorry if saying it wasn't the right thing. But I was under the impression that we could both feel it, and it seemed safer to have it out in the open. I don't know. I feel like, if we ignored it, it could become this big…thing. And it doesn't have to be a thing. I thought it would be best to be honest, so you could make an informed decision about whether you want to stay. I didn't say it because I want you to go.'

'But isn't it complicated, me staying, now that we've said that?'

'It doesn't have to be. Because we're grown-ups here, Madeleine. Right? So there's a spark. You're Jake's sister. I'm hardly going to act on it.'

She wasn't sure how much of what she was feeling was showing on her face. But she was a little affronted, and she would be surprised if Finn wasn't perfectly aware of that fact right about now.

'Come on. I have six-month-olds. *Two* of them. I'm basically desperate for your help. I love Jake and I would never do anything that would risk my oldest and strongest friendship. You're like family to me, Madeleine. I love you and I want you to be safe. But I don't want more than that. I didn't think you did either.'

'I don't!' she said, her voice spiky with indignation. 'Why do you suddenly think that I do?'

'I don't. But everything is so awkward this morning and I just want everything to go back to normal. God, it's never this hard with Jake. Why can't it just be that simple with us?'

'Um, these?' she suggested, glancing down at her chest.

'No,' Finn said, meeting her eyes with a glare that caused a crease between his eyebrows. 'Don't accuse me of that. That's not fair.'

'Come on.' She forced a nonchalant shrug. 'It's just a body. You said yourself; it's just attraction.'

'Actually, I don't think I did say that.' That frown again.

'What then?'

'I'm pretty sure that I said we had *chemistry*. And your body…' he gestured towards her while his eyes remained fixed determinedly on hers '…lovely as I'm sure it is, is not chemistry.'

'Attraction. Chemistry. Whatever,' she said, trying to dismiss his words. But if what he felt for her wasn't based on how she looked, then she wasn't sure where that left them. He was easy to write off if he was only interested in how she looked. She had had plenty of practice dealing with that, after all. But chemistry was something else. Chemistry was something linking them. Something bringing them together. Something mutual. And it was definitely harder to ignore than attraction.

The worst thing was, he was right. There was something between them. She didn't want it to be there, and she didn't like it being there. But it was there, and she didn't know how to make it go away.

Pretty much her whole adult life, she'd only been interested in relationships where she knew the score because she was the one making up the rules. She'd dated guys who were pretty and shallow and uninteresting, because she knew that she could drop them without a second thought when they disappointed her. Which they invariably did. And now here was Finn. Totally honourable. Totally out of bounds. Totally confusing her.

Hart started to grizzle, growing bored of burying his hands in the sand, and Madeleine picked him up, standing and bouncing him gently on her hip, glad for the interruption to what had somehow become an uncomfortably personal conversation.

'Shall we walk for a bit?' she asked Finn, smiling at Hart as he quietened with her and made grabs at her hair and her earrings.

'So we're just calling it quits on that conversation?' Finn asked, looking at her sceptically.

'We are,' she confirmed. Though she had her suspicions that this chemistry wasn't going to fade helpfully into the background and allow her to concentrate on—say—her childcare responsibilities or job-hunting or finding somewhere to live.

'I'm feeling restless,' she announced, lifting Hart into the air and then planting a kiss on his forehead, pulling faces at him before parking him higher on her hip. 'Can we walk? Please?'

'We can go for a walk,' Finn confirmed,

standing so that he could look her in the eye. 'But we started this conversation last night. And it feels like leaving it unfinished is adding to the tension here. If we keep walking away from it, it's going to become a thing.'

It was her turn to crease her brow, because he was making a lot of assumptions here. Ones that she didn't particularly care for. 'How do you know that talking about it is going to make it go away?'

'Because I'm sure that we've both got very good reasons why we want to make it go away.'

He thought it was just that easy? If it turned out to be, great. She would be delighted. But she couldn't help thinking he was being a little naïve here.

'So we just reason our way out of it?' she asked.

'Exactly.'

She envied his supreme confidence. But she didn't share an ounce of it. 'Not to play devil's advocate here—and I'm not talking about us specifically—but don't you think that if it were that easy to talk your way out of feelings like this, more people would do it? Like, there wouldn't be affairs, or star-crossed lovers. Or, I don't know, inappropriate workplace relationships.'

He rolled his eyes and she knew that he wasn't taking her seriously. 'I'm not talking about other people. I'm talking about us.'

'I noticed,' she said, voice dripping with sarcasm. 'Fine. Let's stop. You're right, it's not getting us anywhere anyway.'

'Good. We'll call a truce,' Finn said to her relief. 'We will ignore everything that we've been talking about this morning because we are grown-ups who know better. But I'm telling you, I can't live with an atmosphere. And if I feel like there is one, we're going to talk about this again.'

Madeleine nodded. 'Fine. But I don't think that's going to happen. We've acknowledged it. We've established that neither of us is interested in pursuing it. We're moving on. Now,' she said, strapping Hart into the pushchair and making moves to fold up the picnic blanket, 'let's go for a walk. I'm not used to lazing in the sunshine.'

He laughed at that. 'As if there's such a thing as lazing with these two around.'

They walked along the South Bank, past the squealing pre-schoolers who were running in and out of the fountains and past pained-looking tourists on the terraces of bars and restaurants, trying to look as if the incessant noise wasn't bothering them. At the foot of the London Eye she stopped and looked up at the pods, rotating so slowly around the centre that it hardly seemed as if they were moving. In her ten years in London, she'd never been up there. Never seen London from a different angle, a different perspective than being stuck right in the middle of it, just trying to get through the day.

'What is it?' Finn asked as she continued to stare up at the giant Ferris wheel.

'Do you think the babies would like it up there, or would they be scared?' she asked Finn, wondering whether she was really asking for the twins or for herself.

'You want to go up?'

She shrugged. 'I don't know. It's a beautiful day. I've been wanting perspective. But this seems a little literal, don't you think?'

He stuck his hands in his pockets and leaned back as he looked at her, his expression thoughtful. 'Perspective is a good thing, however you get it.'

'I'm not sure that going up there is going to find me a new job or a place to live.'

'No, maybe not,' he agreed, 'but I'm pretty sure it's not going to hurt either. So let's go,' he said, pushing the pram towards the Fast Track queue.

'You're just going to queue up?' she asked, laughing with surprise. 'Don't your sort arrange to hire the whole thing, or put on a special event or something?'

He stopped and looked at her, frowning. 'My sort? I practically grew up in your kitchen. How is my sort not your sort?'

She caught up with him, picking up the sunhat that Bella had thrown to the ground as a convenient distraction. 'Um, I don't know. Maybe because when we all left you went off and became a genius and a millionaire?'

'I was always a genius, you know.'

She met his eyes and laughed again at the smirk on his face.

She shoved him gently with her shoulder as she came back to stand beside him. 'You were always a pain, you mean. You were never a genius. You used to burn the toast.'

'And here was me thinking you never noticed me at all.' God, that grin of his really was too much. It spread automatically to her face without her even thinking about it. And it made her want to sway her body closer to his in a way that would be bad for both of their states of mind.

She reined in her libido and tried to keep her body on-message. 'I noticed the smoke alarm going off at regular intervals,' she said. 'It was kind of hard to ignore.'

'I had to get your attention somehow.'

She looked up and met his gaze, neither of them looking away long after the look had turned from friendly to intense to something much more concerning and she knew that, however hard they tried to talk about it or ignore it, this chemistry wasn't going anywhere. The thought sent a shiver through her, and she wasn't quite sure whether it was pleasure or fear.

'Don't tease me.' Her voice dropped to something more serious. Because they couldn't keep bantering like this. They were going to get themselves into trouble.

They had to be more careful. 'You didn't think of me that way back then,' she told him with absolute certainty. 'You couldn't have cared less whether I noticed you or not.'

'God, you're so sure of yourself, aren't you? You can't bear to think that I might remember things differently.'

'Jake would have killed you. Or wanted to, at least.'

He nodded slowly, his eyes still never leaving hers. 'Then it's a good job that Jake could never read my mind.'

'You don't spill your guts to him like you do to me then?'

Finally, the grin was gone. She had got through to him. She saw the defences come back up. 'I don't spill my guts to you.'

'You've not been able to stop talking about this thing between us.'

'Because it's distracting,' Finn said, his voice shorter, spikier. 'It's taking up so much room in my head right now that I don't know how to talk about anything else.'

'Why not just forget it?' she asked.

He placed his hands on his hips, his body

language matching the scowl on his face. 'Because it's important that I don't forget. I know I keep saying that there's this connection between us, Madeleine. And it's true. I feel it. The reason I want to talk about it is because I don't want to give that spark any power. I'm not interested in a relationship. I have the children to think about, I'm still processing a marriage that broke down and nearly took my business down with it, all because I… Look, my life isn't compatible with a relationship. With anyone else, I don't know…maybe I'd be up for something casual. I don't want casual with you. I don't want anything with you because Jake is practically my brother, which makes you family and I don't want to do anything to mess that up.'

God, she hadn't been expecting such a torrent of words. There was too much there to process, standing here amidst a chaotic queue of tourists in the middle of a London summer. She knew that she'd be killing herself trying to remember every word when she was finally alone tonight. But, for now, the gist of it was enough. He was as wary as she was, and he wanted whatever spark this was between them shut down fast. Good. She could get on board with that.

'Then I'm glad we're on the same page because I don't want anything either, casual or otherwise, Finn. It sounds like you're afraid I'm going to jump you. Or seduce you or something. For the record, I'm not interested in a relationship with you or anyone else. Now, can we please, *please* stop discussing this?'

He gave her the most intense look for a beat, and then another. And then, when she thought she couldn't bear it any more, he broke into an easy sunny smile and changed the subject. 'When you admit that you are desperate to play the tourist and go on the Eye.'

She was desperate to shut him up. She returned his smile, but couldn't quite convince it to reach her eyes. 'Fine, yes. Let's go.'

'So gracious,' Finn said, pushing the pram further up the ramp as the queue edged close to the embarkation platform.

The pod rose so slowly and smoothly that it was hard to even believe that they were moving unless she looked away from the skyline for a moment, then looked back again to find it that tiny bit further away. The crowded pod—twenty-five of them plus the double buggy—had them wedged into one spot, where for most of the ride up her view was mainly of the back of the six-foot bear of a tourist who had rudely pushed in front of her. She didn't want to look back at the hefty winding gear responsible for keeping nearly five hundred feet of Ferris wheel in the air. And it didn't take long for her to realise that actually she had been pretty happy down on the ground, untroubled by thoughts of how sturdy that engineering really was.

But as the pod crested the top of the wheel and the bear of a man in front of her moved to another part of the pod, her cynicism fell away. The early summer sunshine flooded them with light and suddenly London was glorious beneath them, the river a living, moving ribbon through the landmarks of the city that had become so familiar that she'd stopped seeing it. From up here, she couldn't believe that she didn't spend her day looking around herself in wonder at the city where she got to live. And then, when she looked to her left, there were the Houses of Parliament.

She bit her lip, letting her hand rest on the glass as she took in the sight of the seat of British politics, the location of so many key moments in the history of the country. She'd dreamed of those Gothic buildings all through her degree course. She had been so sure that that was where she was headed. She'd be up close with the people making those decisions, holding them to account and providing the checks and balances that ensured a fair and accountable system of government.

But instead she was up here. Looking down on the Palace of Westminster like the tourist she would be if she turned up there now. From this height, it looked like a model. A toy. It might as well not be real for all the chance she had of working there now.

Finn's hand rested on her shoulder and she jumped, realising she'd forgotten that he was there. She had been so wrapped up in her dreams and her lost hopes that she'd forgotten she was meant to be helping him out. That was the whole point of her being here.

'Are the babies okay?' she asked, angling to try and see them in the pushchair.

'They're zonked. They must like the movement of the wheel. What's going on with you? You're miles away.'

She couldn't help a quick glance out of the pod towards Parliament before she answered. 'I'm fine. I'm great.'

Finn frowned. Really, this mind-reading ability was getting kind of annoying. 'You haven't taken your eyes off Big Ben for a full five minutes.'

God, why did he have to be so perceptive?

'You studied politics, right? I'm sure Jake told me that.'

Madeleine made a noise that she hoped sounded vague enough not to prompt any questions. But Finn was a talker. How had she not noticed that before? Because she'd never given herself a chance to. She'd dodged conversations with him for as long as she could remember.

'You know, the more you avoid my questions the more curious I'm going to get.'

She glanced up at him, finally taking her eyes off the view.

'I'm not going to push you. But if you want to talk, I'm right here.'

Right here.

He was. So close. The crush of people around them only served to push them closer to one another.

'I know.' But she couldn't talk about that. About university or her career—or lack of it. The spectre of what might have been. A weird sadness for how things might have turned out. It was too painful to touch. Especially with him; he had a way of looking at her that made her feel raw. Exposed. She wasn't going to volunteer to peel off another layer of skin for him.

She wrapped her arms around her body as she turned deliberately away from the river and pasted a sunny smile on her face. She waited for it to reflect on Finn's lips, but he just kept staring at her in that unnerving way. Well, he was either a sociopath or he could see straight through her fakery. At this point she couldn't be sure which of those two possibilities was the scarier.

'What do you want to do next?' Finn asked, and she breathed a sigh of relief at the change of subject. 'We could find somewhere for our picnic. Or choose one of the restaurants or cafés we walked past, if you've changed your mind.'

'No, a picnic sounds good. If these monsters wake up, I think I'll be glad of the lack of people staring.'

'Oh, people can still stare in the park,' he informed her with a laugh. 'Especially if they both get going.'

'Well, that's something to look forward to.'

She followed Finn as he pushed the pram out of the pod and down the ramp, and they weaved their way through the disorientated tourists standing around the exit gate. With barely a clipped ankle, he had them away from the crowds and exploring the streets winding away from the river.

'Where are we headed?' she asked as she lost track of where they were.

'I heard there's a little park down this way,' he said. 'I thought it might be quieter than staying by the river. You don't mind?'

A literal change of scenery was exactly

what she needed after ruminating on the failure of her career. And her failure to come to terms with it in the decade that had passed since.

When they reached the gardens, she let out a long breath. Emerald grass was dappled with sunshine filtered through lush trees. Spring flowers lingered in the shady spots and the grass was yet to be scorched by a harsh city summer. But, most delicious of all, it was silent. Somehow, in the walk away from the riverside, the bustle and noise of the city had fallen away, leaving only a blissful quiet. She heard herself let out a long deep breath and for the first time since she had arrived on Finn's doorstep, tense and angry, she felt her shoulders relax.

'Oh, my God, this place is amazing,' Madeleine said, dropping to the grass and lying flat on her back before she could even be bothered to get the picnic blanket out. Finn laughed and dropped to sit beside her, his forearms resting casually on his knees.

'Starved of grass?' he asked with another laugh.

'God, I didn't even realise I was.' She feathered the blades between her fingers, letting them tickle against her palm and slip through her hands. 'And silence. I can't believe how quiet this place is. How did you find it? Tell me your secret.'

She kept her eyes closed as she realised how intimate that sounded. There was safety in closed eyes. But vulnerability too. If he was watching her, she didn't know it. She assessed her body, trying to sense whether his eyes were on her. But all she could feel was the sunshine, hot on her heavy limbs, and she decided she could live with that. She didn't need to know if he was looking at her. She was happy not knowing, just soaking up the heat and the light and feeling the ghosts of the past twenty-four hours melting away.

She heard Finn stand, then the flap and rustle of the picnic blanket. Then he was lying beside her again. And with the tension gone from her body, awareness crept in.

They had lain side by side in the sand-pit before. But they had been protected by the noise of the crowds along the riverside cafés and the squeals of children playing in the fountains. In this private garden they had lost that safety net. They had left home that morning for the protection of being out in public, to escape the heightened tensions of their temporarily shared home. But now they were alone again.

She opened her eyes and glanced across at Finn, only to find him propped up on one elbow, watching her as if she were a puzzle he was trying to solve.

'What?' she asked, suddenly self-conscious, lifting herself onto her elbows. Too late, she realised what that did to her chest, but Finn's eyes never headed south of her nose.

'Nothing.'

'Then why are you staring?'

'I'm looking, not staring.'

'Said the serial killer.'

Finn laughed and rolled his eyes. 'You're not what I was expecting.'

'How can I surprise you? You've known me for ever.'

'You've known me for just as long. You think I couldn't surprise you?'

She thought back to last night. Not the

mistaken assumption she had made, but the way that he had reacted to it. No judgement. No offence taken. Just concerned with making her feel safe. The whole focus of his quite brilliant brain directed at making her feel secure and unthreatened and safe. And it had taken some time to kick in but here, in the sunshine, she was happy. She knew her problems would be waiting for her when they walked out of this park, but in this quiet oasis she was calm and content.

Just as she thought she might actually drop off to sleep Finn's phone rang, surprising her out of her sleepiness. She watched as he dug in his pocket to retrieve it and guessed the identity of the caller from the slight crease on his brow.

'Caro, hey, how are you?' he said, and Madeleine turned away, knowing that it would be rude to eavesdrop, but not sure what else she could do when they were the only people here.

'No, they're asleep,' Finn said, and she knew that Caro must be asking about the babies. Finn angled the phone towards the pair of them sleeping in their pram, and

Madeleine realised that they must be video calling. She wondered whether Caro could see her lying there on the grass. Whether Finn had told her that she was staying with them. It didn't matter, she reminded herself. She was just the help. Even if Caro did see her, it was up to Finn to let her know what was going on. Or not.

God, how had she even got herself down this train of thought? she asked herself. She sat up, trying to shake off the thoughts.

But, now that it had occurred to her, she couldn't help but see this situation as an outsider would—the two of them alone in a park, the kids asleep, lying on a picnic blanket. If that were her husband…

Ex-husband, she reminded herself. Finn was Caro's ex-husband, and had been for a year.

Why did that seem to matter to her all of a sudden? Both she and Finn couldn't have been clearer with one another that what they had was nothing more than a practical arrangement between friends. Not even friends. Between two people who cared for Jake and were happy to do him a favour.

So why did she feel so uncomfortable

now? Why did she feel the need to explain herself? She heard Finn saying his goodbyes and stared at a flowerbed across the park, trying to look completely uninterested in Finn talking to his ex-wife.

'Sorry about that,' he said as he slid his phone back into his jeans pocket.

'No need to apologise,' Madeleine said, probably a little too quickly for someone who was not meant to be listening to his conversation.

'She hates it when they're asleep when she calls,' Finn said. 'She'll probably call back again in a bit if she can.'

'It must be hard for her. She must really miss them. Hard for you too.'

He sighed. The smile she was used to seeing on his face was missing.

'Her work is so important. But… I can't lie… This wasn't how I expected my marriage to turn out.'

'Were you sad when it ended?'

She wasn't sure what made her ask. Of course he had been sad. No one ended a marriage unscathed.

'Sad, but not surprised.'

Madeleine held her breath, with the distinct impression that Finn needed to talk about this. She stayed silent, curious about whether he was going to open up to her again. What would it mean if he did? They had only spent a day in one another's company, and already she had shared more about herself with Finn than she had with anyone else for years. If he was sharing too, then this wasn't an arrangement any more. They were…friends.

'I knew it was coming,' Finn said. 'The longer we were together, the more unhappy she became. I think when she decided to go, it was a relief for her. I…didn't find it easy,' Finn said, and Madeleine winced at what she guessed was a hell of an understatement.

'Did you try—' Madeleine started, then stopped herself. It was really none of her business. Even if they really were friends, it was surely an unwelcome degree of intrusion.

'By the time she told me she was going, she didn't want to try,' he said. 'Seems I used up all my chances without even realising it.' His voice was tinged with regret. 'It's not her fault,' he continued, and Madeleine could sense the false brightness in his voice. 'I wasn't a good husband. I worked too much. I never made time for her. I've spent my life building up the business, determined that…determined my life would be different now, and I didn't want to take the time out of the office to make sure that that was the most important thing to her too. I guess, in the end, I chose the business over her, and it nearly cost me everything.'

Madeleine looked at him for a moment and got the impression that he was expecting her censure. Well, he might be opening up about his guilty feelings, but he could keep on looking. She wasn't here to judge him.

'Marriage is complicated. I'm sure you tried your best.'

'That's the thing, though. I didn't. I knew I wasn't, and Caro knew it too. We were even able to cite it in the papers as unreasonable behaviour.'

She gave him a grim smile. 'You worked hard for that business. Your hard work changed your life. That's got to be a pretty difficult habit to break. But look at you now. Devoted dad. Here with me, not in the office, because you're determined to find the right person to take care of your kids. Looks like you've got your priorities right at the moment.'

'That's different,' he said, frowning, as if he was determined not to accept her assessment of the situation. 'They're my kids; it's not a choice, it's just what I have to do.'

'Plenty of people wouldn't do what you're doing. I'm not commenting on you and Caro. It's not my place, and no one can understand what a marriage is really like just from looking in from the outside. I'm not going to go along with your pity party. You're a good dad, a good person, Finn.'

He grimaced, but let the matter drop.

'Are we going to eat before these kids wake up?' he asked, breathing out a sigh of relief at the change of subject. He had never meant to get so heavy with Madeleine. And he *never* talked about what had happened with Caro. But after what had happened last night, after he had seen Madeleine so vulnerable, after she had shared a little of her past with him, it seemed wrong to hold out on her. Sharing a bit of his life made them equals again.

But it made them something more too—confidantes? Intimates? Whatever it was, she wasn't just his friend's sister any more. They were something to one another now, something that existed outside of their relationships with Jake.

He dug into the picnic bag and brought out cheeses and ham, salad and bread. There was a flask of coffee in there, and a bottle of Sicilian lemonade.

Madeleine swung her legs around, sitting cross-legged with the sun behind her, her hair highlighted by its rays and her skin glowing from the warmth of the day.

'So, how *is* the nanny hunt going?' she asked.

He narrowed his eyes, stopped short by her question. Was she trying to find a way out of their arrangement? Admittedly, it had already got more personal than he had planned, but she had only been there a day. And this mutual attraction that they had both acknowledged and then pledged to determinedly ignore had complicated matters beyond recognition. But that didn't mean that he wanted her to leave. She was staying with him because she had nowhere else to go. He had promised that he would look out for her, and he hated the thought that she might be making plans to leave because of everything that had happened over the past twenty-four hours.

'I've been speaking with the agency,' he said, wishing he could smooth the crease he could feel in his forehead, but not quite managing to get his muscles to co-operate. 'They're going to send some people over this week for interviews. It would be great if you could sit in, actually, if you don't mind?'

The crease in her brow at this request reflected his own, and he wished that he could see inside her head and work out what was going on in there. Last night had brought them closer, there was no denying that. But there was also absolutely no denying that she still had some very substantial protective barriers in place. She might have shown him more of herself than she had planned to last night, but she was making up for it now with reinforced defences.

'I... I don't know if that's a good idea. I

don't know anything about being a nanny. I don't even know much about you or the kids.'

'I trust you. I trust your judgement. It would just be nice to have someone to talk it over with. If you don't mind.'

It was the sort of subject that he should talk over with his wife, except she had left him and the country as soon as she could be rid of him. Even the lure of their two children hadn't been enough to stop her wanting to get away from him. What he'd told Madeleine had been true. He hadn't tried hard enough to save his marriage. He had never put Caro first. He had been a spectacularly bad husband, and he couldn't blame Caro for wanting to put the whole catastrophe behind her.

But even he couldn't have imagined how devastating losing her would prove to be. For the first time ever he had thought that he had a stable home. For seven years they had lived in their beautiful house with their perfect life and full fridge and plans for the future. And then, all of a sudden, it was pulled from under him.

He'd lost it all: Caro, his home. Very

nearly his business, if he'd not been able to secure the funding that they'd needed for the new premises in time.

Now he had the kids to focus on, he could tell himself that he didn't even miss her. And he didn't. Sure, sometimes he missed having another adult to speak to at the end of the day—he loved sharing the kids' firsts and milestones with her over video calls—but he didn't really miss her. And when their marriage was falling apart, all he could think about was how he was going to ensure that the financial consequences didn't reduce him to the poverty he had spent his life running from. What did that say about him—that he was more concerned about his bank balance than about trying to save his relationship?

It only went to show how much he'd let her down. It had been a long time since he'd been in love with Caro.

They'd married young, when his business had first started to boom and he'd realised he didn't have the skills or the experience or the connections to navigate the world he was suddenly living in. Caro had all that—had grown up in that world. She'd shared it with him, and he had honestly loved her, at the start. But as the years had gone on, and he had found himself further and further out of his depth, he had to work harder and harder. Spend more and more hours at the office. And what he'd had with Caro had…died. Because he had neglected it. And she had tired of the world of CEOs and easy money that she had grown up in and decided she wanted to do something more…worthy.

He looked over to where Madeleine was helping herself to the picnic and was hit with that stab of attraction that had been present since the moment that he had opened the door to her the day before.

If they hadn't had that misunderstanding yesterday evening, would he have acknowledged his attraction to her? Would he have ignored it—pretended it wasn't there? Or would he have flirted with her? Played with that chemistry, and seen where it might take them?

With Jake's sister? he reminded himself. No, he wouldn't. He couldn't. She was as off-limits today as she had been yesterday. He had to remember that. But her culottes had slid up her legs, showing smooth, toned calves, and he physically ached with the need to reach out a hand and feel the softness of her skin, the firmness of the muscle. He flexed his fingers and tried to concentrate on his food. But for once he could barely taste it. He was more interested in the curve of her lip and the close of her eyelids as she tasted an olive. The slide of her finger into her mouth as she sucked them clean.

He stifled a groan. That really wasn't helping matters.

'What?' Madeleine asked, opening her eyes and catching him watching her.

He opened his mouth to tell her *Nothing*, but no sound came out. Instead he held her gaze and watched as her expression shifted from quizzical to interested to knowing. He knew that what he was thinking must be written all over his face. But he had told her yesterday how he felt. It would be dishonest of him to try and hide it from her now. At least that was what he told himself so that he didn't feel he had to tear his eyes away. Not just yet. He just wanted another moment.

'Finn…?'

He waited in silence to see where that sentence was going. But it seemed either Madeleine didn't know or didn't want to share it with him, because her voice faded out. Her eyes dropped too. To his lips, and then back up again.

Her lower lip slipped between her teeth and she bit down, and he knew that they were thinking the exact same thing. How would it feel to press his mouth against her lips? To feel the slide and the power of them beneath his own? To taste and to test? To press against her until they were stretched out on the grass, the sun hot on their bodies as they explored beneath their clothes?

The cry of a baby behind him brought that stifled groan to life, and Madeleine took a breath as she glanced over at the pushchair.

Maybe it was for the best, he considered as he followed her gaze and saw Hart stirring.

And maybe he was going to spend the rest of the day wondering exactly where that look might have taken them if they hadn't been interrupted. He had a feeling he knew which way that was going to pan out. And it didn't look good for his peace of mind.

CHAPTER SEVEN

OH. MY. HAD that been a moment? Had they just had a moment? One second she'd thought she was just picking at some antipasti, and the next Finn was looking at her like he wanted to eat her. In a really, *really* good way. He had watched her lips until her eyes had been drawn to his mouth too, and just as her body had begged her to find out what it would feel like—

Hart had woken up, and the moment was gone. Because she was not ready to deal with how much she'd wanted that kiss to happen.

Not like this. Not with Finn.

Because she knew what she wanted from her relationships. She wanted predictability, and the balance of power firmly on her side. She wanted to be able to walk away when she decided it was over because that was the only way that she knew how to handle this stuff. To be fair to herself, it was the only way that she had tried. Maybe, if she'd wanted to, she could have had a go at something different and made that work too. But she never had, because that meant opening herself up to getting hurt and she had precisely zero interest in doing that. Not with Finn, or with anyone else.

But when Finn looked at her like that—like he wanted to eat her, to consume her, to make her a part of him—she wanted to find out what that felt like. She wanted to give herself over to it and care precisely nothing about the consequences. Because she was pretty sure that the not knowing was going to kill her. The not knowing, and the being so damn close that she could practically taste him. Which was why she had to get up off this blanket and start walking and stop thinking before she did something she would regret later.

That night, Madeleine slipped between the cool cotton sheets and stretched out her feet, pointing her toes until she was sure that some part of her foot would just snap completely. After the babies had woken up they had played in the park with them for nearly an hour, pushing swings and taking gentle turns of the roundabout, rocking horses and adventures in diggers.

And then, with the picnic bag empty—and the coffee flask dangerously so—they had headed away from the green oasis in search of sugar and caffeine to keep them fuelled until the babies decided that they'd had enough of exploring and wanted to sleep in the pram. She wished she'd realised before she'd started how many miles you could cover with babies who would only sleep on the move. She couldn't have been more grateful when they'd woken and informed them—at some considerable volume, that it was time to go home now, please.

Once they were through the doors of the house, it had been a whirlwind of steamed veg and finger food and sterilising bottles. Bathing naked babies and wriggling them into Baby-gros and humming nursery rhymes.

By the time that she and Finn had collapsed in front of the TV she couldn't have cared less that they might have had a moment back there on the picnic blanket. All she wanted was spadefuls of the mac and cheese that Finn had found in the freezer, and the sweet, sweet oblivion of sleep. Neither of them had managed more than half an hour of the movie they'd stuck on before giving up any pretence that they would be awake later than nine o'clock.

It felt as if her head had barely hit the pillow before the crying began, but a glance at the time on the front of her phone told her that it had been a couple of hours. Turned out midnight really was the witching hour. She could leave Finn to it, she supposed—they were his kids currently screaming the house down. But she was here to help him out and what was even the point of these awkward living arrangements if she wasn't doing that?

She stumbled out of bed and threw on her cardigan, pulling on socks in anticipation of the tile floors downstairs. She pulled her hair into a ponytail high on her head, opened her door and nearly crashed into Finn, who was holding a wailing Bella on his shoulder and a tear-stained Hart on his hip.

'Oh, thank God,' Finn said, shoving Hart in her direction. 'Would you take him? He's settled for now but I just can't get him down.'

'I don't—'

But her reply was cut short by the arrival of Hart on her hip and she didn't have any choice but to hold on. He gave her an uncertain look and his bottom lip wobbled, but no tears were forthcoming for now.

'Is there something wrong with Bella?' she asked as she followed him and Bella's cries down the hall.

'Teeth? Wind? Existential angst? Your guess is as good as mine at this point.'

'How long has she been crying?'

'An hour? Half an hour? A week…?'

'Do you want me to take her?'

Finn's face creased as he peered at Bella, and Madeleine could see the ruminations behind his eyes as he tried to work out what was wrong.

'Maybe she's sick of me,' he said with a shrug before completing some sort of superpower twin manoeuvre which resulted in her finding that she was now holding Bella and Finn was bouncing Hart.

'What do I do?' Madeleine asked, aware that her eyes were widening in alarm as Bella's volume picked up a notch and the bouncing and patting that had worked with Hart the night before only seemed to make things worse.

'This…this is the part where we pace,' Finn said, heading past her door to the end of the corridor, bouncing and patting as he went. And pace they did. Long past her feet hurting. Long after her back started to ache and her shoulders started to burn. She saw half an hour tick by on her phone. Then an hour. By the time that Bella stopped screaming, they had moved their pacing down to the kitchen so that the adults could at least dose with caffeine to get through what was feeling like an endless night and the babies could spit out the lovingly pre-pared formula that Finn had somehow managed to make one-handed.

When Bella finally exhausted herself in Finn's arms and Hart was asleep on her shoulder, Madeleine was left with a deli-ciously heavy bundle snuggled into her as she collapsed onto the sofa in the open-plan area. Finn leaned back against the kitchen island, pinching the bridge of his nose before rubbing a hand across his forehead.

'I can't believe you've been doing this on your own,' Madeleine said.

'It's not always like this,' Finn said with a wry smile. 'Wait here. I'll put Bella to bed and come back for Hart.'

Madeleine snuggled deeper into the corner of the sofa and her eyes were just starting to close when she heard Finn's bare feet padding across the tiles of the kitchen floor.

'I'm sleeping here,' she mumbled without opening her eyes. 'Possibly for a week.' She heard his smile in his little huff of breath. Didn't even need to crack open an eyelid to see the lines around his eyes that he always got when he grinned.

'Let me take him,' Finn said, and her shoulder was suddenly cold where Hart had been snuggling and she heard the gentle swish-swish of his swinging chair.

'If you're sleeping, I'm sleeping,' Finn said at last, when they had both finally released their held breath. 'Budge up.'

She lifted her feet so that he could collapse at the other end of the sofa, and it was only when her thighs started to ache that she realised she really hadn't thought this through. She lowered them slowly and felt heat spark when Finn's hand cupped her ankle and guided her feet onto his thighs.

'God, you really need a nanny,' she said, trying to think of any topic of conversation that would distract her from the electric feel of his hands resting on her. Suddenly, her ankles were the most sensitive part of her body and she could feel the heat of each of his fingertips as they gently rested against her.

He's not even thinking about it, she told herself. *He's literally only touching you because you refused to give up the sofa.*

Except now one fingertip was tracing a feather-light circle around her ankle bone, so slowly, so gently that she suspected that Finn didn't even know that he was doing it. Had no idea that he was driving her so insane with the gentlest of touches.

'I've scared you off, haven't I?' he said. 'You're going to pack your bags first thing in the morning.'

'No, not that,' she said, trying to keep her mind on the subject of nannies and their arrangement, and definitely not on the sparks of heat that she could feel radiating out from his hands on her. From the feel of hard muscle beneath her feet. 'You must be desperate for someone who knows what they're doing, that's all. I don't feel like I was much help tonight.'

His grip on her ankle was suddenly firmer, the wandering fingertips that had been driving her so insane were still, and she could feel that the hardness in his body went beyond that. She had annoyed him. Perfect.

'Why do you do that, Maddie? You did great tonight. I hate that you won't acknowledge how capable you are.'

She cracked an eye open at last, trying to read the expression on his face from the half-light of the lamp in the corner of the room.

'Okay, I won't say it again. It's no big deal.' She shut her eyes, tried to get the swimmy, heavy feeling of nearing sleep back into her muscles but it was gone, and she was angry at Finn for that. It was bad enough that she was awake in the middle of the night. Worse that he was annoying her so much that she couldn't even get the sleep she so desperately wanted.

'Don't,' Finn said, holding onto her as she went to swing her ankles off the sofa and sit up. 'I'm sorry,' he carried on in hushed tones. 'I didn't mean to criticise.' The stroking fingertips were back, driving her insane, and really she knew that that was reason enough to take herself off to bed. But… But. But she was a complete idiot and clearly needed her head examined, and it felt so good to have his skin so near to hers that she felt herself relaxing back, her eyes drifting shut again.

She could feel the intimacy settle over them like a blanket, shutting out the real world. They were the only two people awake in London. She was sure of it. Never mind that she had been out in this city at every hour of the day and night and never found it sleeping. She was quite sure that she and Finn were the only people in the world right now. As if they had slipped through some sort of wormhole brought about by screaming and pacing and fallen into a universe where no one but the two of them existed.

'I didn't mean to snap.' She sighed. Finn's hands stilled and she let out an involuntary mew of displeasure and nudged him with her toes. Her feet ached. Her calves ached. Her toes ached. She'd had no idea that it was possible to walk so far without leaving the house. The circles around her ankle bone resumed, each one unwinding her a little looser, each one undoing her a little more, so when Finn asked, 'What happened?' she didn't have the energy to throw up her usual barriers. The words fell out of her.

'A professor, the last year of my university course. I thought he was taking an interest because I showed promise. I thought the grades I was getting were because I was working hard. But it was all a play. It was all to get me where he wanted me. To get what he wanted from me.'

The hand on her ankle stilled, and she nudged him again. If he stopped, if they returned to real life, there was no way that she could talk about this. The circles came back, and so did her words.

'When he made it clear what he really wanted… When he locked his door and stood in front of it so that I couldn't escape, I finally worked it out. God, what kind of journalist was I going to be if I couldn't even see that coming? I managed to get out of there, and that's when it all fell into place. It was never my work that he saw. It was my body. He thought that he could just take it. That I would hand it over. Well, I didn't. I wouldn't. I walked out of university and I never went back and I lost my career because of it. Well, the career that I wanted. That I might have had. Except I'll never know now, will I? I'll never know if I could have had that career, because everything I know about my ability has been cast into doubt. I never got a single grade that I don't ask myself whether it was for my insight and understanding and thorough research. Or whether it was just someone wanted to get a better look at my boobs.'

Finn was quiet, still for a long moment, and when he spoke his voice was ice. 'You should kill him.'

She gave a wry smile at his instinctive response to protect her. 'Too late. I thought about it, but a heart attack beat me to it. Two years ago. Glowing obits in all the broadsheets.'

'You could dig him up and kill him again.' The words were ground out, shocking her with their carefully harnessed rage. She opened her eyes and the expression on his face startled her. She had never seen his features contorted into such anger. Every line of his face was hard. His jaw was a slash of muscle beneath the hollows of his cheeks. The bones above were stark lines caught by the light from the lamp. The creases around his eyes owed nothing to laughter now. They were deep and harsh.

She sat up, her feet sliding under his leg now, her knees bent as she hugged herself smaller, brought herself closer to him.

He shook himself and she watched as he forced some of the tension from his face. When his eyes met hers she wanted to hide from the raw intensity there, but then her hand was on his face and she couldn't look away.

He gripped her other hand hard, and she could feel him shaking. 'I am so, so sorry that that happened to you,' he said.

His other hand came to rest on top of hers, trapping it against his jaw. 'If you want to talk more about it, I'm here. I want to help—just tell me what I can do.'

She shrugged. 'There's not much more to tell. And there's nothing you can do.' His grip on her hand softened and she let her body follow, resting against the sofa cushions, still tucked into her little protective ball. But when she leaned against the sofa Finn's shoulder was right there and in a breath, no more than two, her cheek was resting against it, drawing the heat from it. When his arm circled around her back to tuck her more firmly into his side, she didn't fight it. With her toes tucked under his thigh and his arms a hard band of bone and muscle around her back and her waist, his shoulder the pillow under her cheek, she was surrounded by him.

If she dared open an eyelid, he would be her entire field of vision. He was the firm support under her head and the gentle strokes on her aching calves. He was the heavy weight on her feet and the rise and fall that was lulling her into sleep. He was the gentle huffs of breath, the slight movement as it nudged her hair.

The wormhole universe that they had created had shrunk around them until the only way that they could both exist inside it was by curling up tight. Tangling limbs around one another. Sharing a space that only seconds before had only been big enough for one. And for the first time in as long as she could remember she felt still. And quiet. And as sleep dragged her under she didn't care what she was going to think about all this in the morning. All she cared about was the aching perfection of their universes merging and colliding, and finding peace there.

CHAPTER EIGHT

MADELEINE WAS IN his arms.

She was practically in his lap. Her feet were still tucked under his leg, her cheek on his shoulder. One hand rested on his chest.

He had no idea how long they had been asleep, but the sky was lightening and Hart's swing had stopped moving. The dark circles had started to fade under Madeleine's eyes, and it took more self-control than he realised he had not to stroke the skin there, to try and soothe her tiredness.

He could kick himself. It was his fault that she was so exhausted. As if she didn't have enough going on in her life right now with losing her job and her flat, he had added sleep deprivation and crying babies onto her list of things to worry about. He should have just given her a place to stay, no questions asked, no strings attached. That was what she needed. That was what she deserved. Except he knew now that she wouldn't have taken it. Jake must have known too, and he silently thanked his friend for looking out for Madeleine in a way that he hadn't known how. From the moment that she had walked into his home she had thrown up walls between them so obvious that there hadn't been any point offering to do this another way.

But last night she hadn't shut him out. She had let him in and told him something that he had a sneaking suspicion she hadn't told anyone else about before. And then she had curled into him and slept and he had held onto her and sworn that he would keep her safe. It didn't matter that she was already gently snoring by then. It didn't even matter than she had been doing a pretty good job of keeping herself safe. He was there for her now. Whenever she needed him. Whatever she wanted from him. He would be there.

Except… Except how could he promise that?

With his failed marriage and the business that was desperate for him to return. With two babies who would always, absolutely and without exception, *always* come first. He had let Caro down, had been too distant, too absent, too distracted. What there was of him to share hadn't been enough for her, and that was even before the twins had come along. Now there was less of him than ever, and he wanted Madeleine to have more than that. She deserved someone who was devoted to her. Who she could rely on. Not someone who was already pulled in more directions than he knew how to handle.

But that was before he had woken up to her curled against his chest and tucked into his body. Now all his resolve was in very great danger of flying out of the window. What he wanted, more than anything, was to run his hands up the soft jersey covering her legs. To start at the delicate bone on her ankle that he hadn't been able to leave alone last night. To stroke up over those strong, toned calves that he knew must be aching from their afternoon walking along the South Bank, and then the hours that they had spent pacing last night. He wanted to sweep his hands up over her back. To stop at the nape of her neck and pull her closer, to tip her face up to his and...

'Finn? This is...'

Delicious? Incredible? Perfect?

'Awkward,' she finished, pulling herself away and tucking herself into a ball at the other end of the sofa. 'I'm sorry,' she carried on, wrapping her arms around her knees.

And he could see every single barrier that had dropped between them last night go flying back up. And he couldn't even resent it, because she needed those barriers. They both did, because his own were faltering badly and one of them needed to be doing the sensible thing here: nipping this chemistry in the bud before it could get out of control and hurt one or both of them.

Since she had first walked in here, they had both known that there was something between them. The way that they had avoided one another over the past few years, he wondered if they had known it longer even than that. But they also knew that it was completely out of bounds. It wasn't something that either of them was going to be permitted to explore. It was something to avoid. To push into a tiny, tiny space in his mind and ignore until he forgot about it. Simple as that.

'No, don't be sorry,' he said, standing and turning to the kettle. Anything for a distraction while he tried to compose himself and stuff his feelings into the tiny box where they belonged. Somehow both the babies were still sleeping. No wonder, he supposed, having been awake half the night. If they could keep it up long enough for him to have his first drink of the day then that would be just perfect.

When he turned back round with a cup of tea in each hand, Madeleine was perching on the edge of the sofa, cardigan wrapped tight around her. It didn't take a genius to work out that she was on the defensive. That cardigan, as deliciously soft as it had been against his skin when he had blinked awake a few minutes ago, was now being deployed as armour.

How could he blame her? If she was feeling anything like as conflicted as he was this morning then she would need it.

He glanced at his phone and flicked through his email, still not ready to look at Madeleine. Ah. The nanny agency. That was safe ground.

'They've sent me a shortlist,' he said casually, 'of nannies to interview. Are you still okay to help with that? They've said they can send them over tomorrow.'

'Sure. Do you need to go into the office today?'

'Not if I can help it. But I could do with getting a few hours of work in my home office if we can manage it?'

'Sure. Let me know what you need.'

If they could just stay out of one another's way today, maybe this awkwardness would wear off and they would find themselves back to normal tomorrow, he told himself. They'd go into his office and interview nannies and pretend that she hadn't spent the night in his arms, however unusual the circumstances.

Work was the distraction that he needed this morning. The reminder that his business still owed an unimaginably large amount of money for the new office building they had just taken possession of, and he couldn't afford another day away from his computer, Sunday or not.

By tomorrow, Madeleine and the twins would have had a couple of days to get used to one another and he could go into work with a clear conscience. But he couldn't leave Madeleine completely alone with them after the night that they'd had. Not just the lack of sleep, but Madeleine had opened up to him, made herself vulnerable, and it didn't feel right walking out and leaving her to deal with the fallout on her own. He had told her last night that he wanted to be here for her, and he'd meant it.

CHAPTER NINE

TWENTY-FOUR HOURS LATER, and he was pretty sure he had a handle on this Madeleine thing. They'd managed a whole day of being in the apartment together, caring for the babies, with him in and out of his home office, without a single personal conversation or ankle bone in sight. Even the babies had showed pity on them and had only woken for a quick feed in the night and gone straight back to sleep. Seemed everyone was as keen as he was to get them back on an impersonal footing. Well, good. They were both going to be grown-up about this and pretend that nothing had happened.

'How about this for a plan for today?' he suggested as they both sipped a coffee with their breakfast on Monday morning. 'We both take the babies into the office. They're treated like minor celebrities, so all you'll have to do is try and keep track of which one has been taken to which department to be passed around for cuddles. I'll make sure someone brings you a steady supply of coffee, and you can call me in for nappy emergencies. We'll do the interviews there after lunch. Does that sound manageable?'

'If that's what nannying for you is like then I want the job permanently,' she said with a slightly forced polite smile. 'Baby snuggles, no nappies, endless lattes. Sign me up.'

He reflected her creaky grin, wondering where the ease that he had felt before had gone. And then remembered where that ease had led them, and was grateful that they were both back to tiptoeing. 'That deal is just for you. If you tell our interviewees then the deal's off the table.'

'Fine, fine. What time do you need to go in?'

'Can you be ready by half seven?' he asked. 'It'd be good to be at my desk by eight.'

She glanced at the clock on the wall and nodded. 'How do you want to handle the babies? Take one each—divide and conquer? Or assembly line?'

'God, right now I just want to leave them to sleep. If you can give me a hand to get their bags packed we can stick a clean nappy on them the minute before we need to walk out the door. They can party in their pyjamas this morning.'

His kids could go out in their PJs. He could forgo breakfast. But the one thing that he absolutely, definitely could not skip this morning was the cold shower he seemed to be permanently in need of these days.

He watched Madeleine closely as they walked through the lobby of his office building and couldn't help the swell of pride that he felt when he saw the evidence of all he had achieved over the past few years. Seeing Madeleine had reminded him of where he had built all of this from in a way that never seemed to happen during his weekly drinks with Jake. His best friend had been there for him all along. He'd seen the first tiny office space that he had rented. And the larger building when the first investments started coming through. And then he had pored over the plans for this building when his company had outgrown its space again, and he had decided that he needed somewhere bespoke. Something that would help to create the vision he had of his company as somewhere creative and innovative and exciting.

Except that wasn't all he saw when he looked at his place. He also saw the scary number of zeros on his mortgage statement. The one that he wouldn't have needed if he'd managed to hold his marriage together. This was everything that he had worked for, and everything that he stood to lose if he lost control of his personal life a second time. Everything that he stood to lose if he forgot how vital it was to hold Madeleine at a distance and stop himself getting too close.

There were glass open-plan areas, private offices. Different spaces to suit different personalities and moods. A building full of employees relying on him to keep this company afloat, to keep their wages and their own homes safe and secure.

He chatted with the security guard as he

got Madeleine signed in, and nearly lost a twin out of the pushchair before they had even left the lobby. This was always the problem when he brought the babies into work. They were whisked away to be showed off and he could hardly keep track of where they were. He had sold it to Madeleine as an easy morning out, but it was harder to keep track of the babies when they were here than it would be once they were toddling around a busy park by themselves.

'The babies stay in the pushchair until we are upstairs,' Finn said to the guy with a beard and a lumberjack shirt from the design floor who was swooping in to coo at them. 'I promised Madeleine coffee and a comfortable seat before she started having to shepherd them.'

He placed a hand on the small of her back as they crossed the lobby towards the lifts, but pulled it away when he felt her stiffen. So, normal service resumed, he confirmed with a small smile. Good. That was what they both needed. Something had happened between them that night on the sofa. Barriers had come down that he had feared would be impossible to rebuild. She had shared so much with him that he'd thought he had felt the substance of their friendship shift, but it seemed he had been wrong.

This wasn't beyond saving. They could get themselves back somewhere safe, where they could be friends who saw each other occasionally at Jake's family events. Finding the right nanny, and helping Madeleine decide what she wanted to do next, would make that happen even faster.

Madeleine's eyes widened further when he opened the door into his private office, and was it really so terrible to feel such a swell of pride at the expression on her face? It was only as he was hovering at the open glass door into his corner office that he realised how desperate he was for her approval. He stood back and waited while she took a step into the office and then abandoned the pushchair to cross over to the window and look out across the panorama of the London skyline.

'We didn't need to queue for the Eye at all,' she said as her eyes scanned first one way and then the other across the capital.

'We could have just come up here,' Madeleine said with a raised eyebrow and a wry smile.

He laughed and shrugged as he walked over to join her. 'Ah, but you were so keen to do the tourist thing.'

She bumped his shoulder in a friendly way that made him think that their intimacy maybe hadn't disappeared completely with the passage of a too-polite day.

'Seriously, Finn. This is amazing. I hope you're proud, because I am.' She glanced up at him. 'Does that sound really condescending? I'm not sure I care if it does because I mean it. I'm really proud of you. You built all this from scratch while I was writing terrible copy I don't even want to put my name to.'

She must have caught the look that he aimed in her direction at that self-deprecating remark and stopped herself short. Good. He hated that she talked herself down like that. After everything that she had told him over the past few days he wanted to destroy people and places and generally rage out on her behalf. But he couldn't. The only thing that he could do was support her and protect her, even from herself.

'Thank you,' he said, sincerity giving his voice a gravelly edge that surprised him. 'It means a lot that you think that.'

They stood in silence for a few moments more, transfixed by the sight of the city below.

'When we were up in the Eye,' he said, choosing his words carefully, 'you couldn't take your eyes off the Houses of Parliament. That's what you wanted when you were at university, right? Before you had to leave. You wanted to work there.'

He saw surprise on her face, indecision cross her features as she considered him and he prayed to whoever would listen that she would take the leap and trust him with the truth. If she could only be honest with him in the dimmed light of the early hours when they were half delirious with fatigue then this wasn't a friendship. It wasn't anything, really.

She looked him dead in the eye and he held his breath.

'Yes. I wanted to work there. Desperately. As far back as I can remember.'

'And after…'

'After I dropped out of uni I had to accept that it was never going to happen. I missed my chance.'

She took a few long breaths and Finn kept his eyes on the city, giving her the privacy he knew she needed to compose herself. He sensed her straighten her spine, push her shoulders back and he finally glanced over at her.

'It's not too late,' he told her. 'If you want to go back. You could finish your degree.'

She shook her head, her expression fixed and fierce. 'That ship has sailed. It's sunk. It was in flames as it went down. There's no way that I'm going back into that world. Not if it means explaining what happened.'

He laid a hand on her shoulder, wishing he could offer more comfort than that. That he could take her in his arms and protect her as every muscle in his body was urging him to do. But their lives were more complicated than following base urges. There was too much at stake to ignore all the reasons why she needed protecting from him as much as from anyone. What she needed was support, and the only way he could really give her that was by absolutely indisputably refusing to fall in love with her.

'But you still want it,' he said. 'You wouldn't have to tell anyone what happened if you don't want to. Lots of people go back to university.'

She whipped round to look at him. 'And how would I pay for it? It costs ten times what it did when I was there before. Even just repeating the final year is beyond what I can imagine being able to afford. I don't know if the credits from the earlier semesters are even valid any more so I might have to repeat those too. That's before I even get to the question of where I would live and what I would eat. It's impossible, Finn, so please just leave it.'

'Of course it's not impossible. I'll pay for it.'

The look of horror that she shot him hit him straight in the gut, and he recoiled at the anger on her face. He couldn't believe that he had just offered that. It wasn't that he couldn't afford it. His personal finances had been incredibly rocky around the time of his divorce, but some judicious investments had paid off, so that he could breathe easy again at night rather than lying awake, worried that he was bringing two babies into a world that was too precarious for him to be able to guarantee that they would always be well fed and warm.

'God. No, Finn. Absolutely not. That's never going to happen.'

'Why not?' He had helped hundreds, maybe thousands of people go to university by now with his scholarship funds and early intervention programmes he had started early in his career, wanting to see other kids like him follow him up that ladder. Of course he would pay her tuition. Her housing. Whatever she needed.

'Because it would be weird,' Madeleine said. 'And inappropriate. And uncomfortable.'

'Weirder or more uncomfortable than me eating breakfast at your house every day for seven years? Uncomfortable like me wearing Jake's hand-me-down school uniforms? Weird like that time I came on a family holiday with you?'

'That's different,' she said, though they both knew it wasn't. He let it slide this time. 'Anyway, what would we tell Jake?'

'How about to mind his own business?' Finn offered. 'Or we don't tell him anything. Or, um, I don't know, something outrageous like I'm helping you out because you're family and because I want to and I'm in a position to.'

God, there were a lot of 'I's in that sentence, he realised as he stopped speaking. This wasn't about him. It was about her. If he didn't think that it was what she wanted, he wouldn't be pushing this. But there was something about the way that she had looked out the window that made him think that she hadn't given up on this dream just yet. That she still wanted it. That if he could help with the practicalities, clear obstacles from her way, she could go back to it.

'He'd ask awkward questions.'

'Like what? It's not like there's anything going on between us. We have nothing to hide from him. He can ask what he likes.'

His words seemed to freeze out the rest of the world, because he had never in his life heard something that was so completely true and such an enormous lie at the same time. They hadn't slept together, hadn't even kissed. They had both sworn that nothing like that was ever going to happen between them. And yet they were stupid if either of them truly believed that there was nothing going on. Because he was fighting the urge to kiss her every minute they were together. And the urge to fall in love with her every second.

Love? When had he started thinking like that? She had only been back in his life for a few days. For years of his life he had seen her every single day. Eaten meals with her. Gone on holiday with her. Why was this only happening now? Was it just because they were all grown up? Was it because she'd ditched the baggy clothes and raised her eyes from the floor? Was it because he was finally grown up enough to realise just how beautiful she was? Or because he was suddenly divorced and single again for the first time in years?

No, he knew that wasn't it because that was all superficial bull, and if there was one thing that he knew for certain about these feelings that had been growing for Madeleine these last few days it was that they were anything but superficial.

It was that for the first time in his life he was in a room with Madeleine and felt completely her equal. Something that he had never felt when they were growing up. But he had built this business from nothing and he was proud of it. Hadn't realised it was possible to feel prouder, actually, until she had said that she was proud too. And he had never felt so valued, so truly seen as he did standing here with her right now. She didn't see the kid he'd been, as he so often thought that Jake did. She didn't see the CEO he'd become, like everyone else in this building, the failed husband, the man who had lost his home and taken his business to the brink little more than a year ago. She saw the whole person. Everything he had been. Everything he had worked so hard to overcome and become. Everything he still wanted to achieve. No wonder things had been so intense between them. But that wasn't love, or attraction. It wasn't even friendship, he told himself. It was just knowing someone at two extreme moments in their life. He was almost sure that he could convince himself of that.

Hart burbled behind them and he crossed

to the pushchair, his arm brushing against Madeleine's as she followed him and picked up Bella.

'Do you want me to take them somewhere so you can get some work done?' she asked, and he felt the *No* in his gut before it made it to his lips.

'Hang around for a bit,' he said, hoping his voice sounded more level than he felt. He crossed to the double doors of the supply cupboard at the far end of the office and opened them, flicking on the light with his elbow. It was only when he heard the warm chuckle from behind him that he realised how strange it must look.

CHAPTER TEN

'YOU KEEP THE babies in a cupboard?'

Madeleine laughed and took a step closer to investigate. The floor was covered with soft play mats, layered two or three deep over foam tiles locked together on the carpet. Fairy lights and gauzy fabric criss-crossed the walls and draped from the ceiling, and when Finn hit another switch, swirling stars were projected over the whole space and the notes of a nursery rhyme tinkled from a hidden speaker.

'I know, I know,' Finn said. 'It's not ideal. This place was already finished before we found out Caro was pregnant. It was the best I could do in the circumstances. In my defence, at least it's a really big cupboard.'

But she was still smiling as she laid Bella onto one of the play mats—the baby reached straight for one of the squeaky toys and cooed as if she'd been reunited with a dear friend. Madeleine was willing to bet that the cupboard in Finn's office was one of the baby girl's favourite places—and really, who could blame her? Hart had started to reach out for his sister, so Finn put him down on the mat too. Madeleine took a step back to marvel at the cuteness of twin babies in a closet.

'It's a masterpiece,' she told Finn honestly.

'Baby sensory class in a cupboard. I should market it.'

'You'd make a fortune. Another fortune,' she corrected herself, glancing around his office and feeling again that strange mixture of pride and being utterly out of her depth that she'd felt when she'd first walked in here.

He had achieved so much. She'd bitten off her words earlier. Hadn't wanted to turn the conversation back to herself, but the contrast in the direction their lives had taken had never been starker. He had achieved so much. She was homeless and jobless. Had zero prospects for her future. Well, until Finn had proposed some. Paying for her to go back to uni. It was ludicrous. And offered as, what? Some sort of payback for the generosity of her parents? Well, she couldn't accept. Her parents' generosity had nothing to do with her. If he felt some misguided sense of duty, then he could take it up with them or with Jake. She'd never given it a minute's thought.

But she could take it. She let herself think about that for a second. She had no job. No ties. The offer of a generous benefactor. She could go back to university, finish her degree and stop wondering. Stop asking herself what might have been and actually go and *do* something about it.

If only it wasn't Finn making the offer. If only it was some completely disinterested stranger offering her this money to go and follow her dream. Because... Finn. Her feelings for him were anything but disinterested. They were complicated, and growing more so by the day. If she were to take him up on his offer, what would that do to them? What would that do to these feelings that she didn't quite know how to name but was finding increasingly difficult to ignore?

What if there was another way?

When she'd been stuck on the treadmill of rent arrears and copy deadlines, she'd never had a chance to draw breath and work out if there was a way that she could go back to studying. For years she'd hated the thought of having to come into contact with the professor again. But that excuse had died two years ago. He was gone, and she was still here. What if her dreams weren't as dead as she'd thought they might be?

She brought her attention back to the babies on the play mat. This wasn't something that had to be decided now, right away—going back to university or getting a new job. Whatever it was she was going to do next deserved more thought than the reflexive denial she'd just given Finn. She'd had to abandon her dream once already. If she was being given a second chance, she had to at least think about it, however uncomfortable that might make her feel.

'I promise I'll think about your offer,' she said at last. 'It's incredibly generous. I'm sorry that I didn't start by saying that.'

Finn gave her a long intense look that had the colour rising in her cheeks.

'Take all the time you need.'

She blinked once, twice, then turned her attention back to the babies.

'Right,' she told Finn, her tone firm. 'You are meant to be at your desk. I'm going to play with the kids here, but if we're keeping you from working then I'm going to take them on a tour of the building. If we're making too much noise, let me know and I'll get out of your hair.'

The morning passed more quickly than Madeleine had known that time could. By the time that the babies had got bored of their play mat, Finn's assistant had arranged someone to give her a tour of the building, and she'd not needed to do much more than step back and watch as the twins were passed from department to department. A hot cup of coffee had been pressed into her hands whenever they had been empty, and as she passed through the art department the guy with the checked shirt had finally got his cuddle with the babies.

By the time that she had changed two lots of nappies and made up two bottles, fed both babies, burped them and got them back in their pushchair, she realised that she was starving, and had no idea where she could get herself some lunch. She was just looking around for someone to ask when Finn's assistant appeared behind her and let her know that lunch was ready in Finn's office. Cool, problem solved.

When she arrived back on his floor with—somehow, miraculously—two sleeping babies, she was ready to eat her own body weight in cheese. Or, well, whatever culinary delights got sent up to the CEO's office in a company like this.

It was a far cry from the grubby office that she had just been made redundant from. And it made her realise that all the years she had spent in that dingy office with those dingy people had skewed her perception until she had lost sight of what the alternatives were. There were people in this building who loved their job. Who were excited and motivated to get to their desk in the morning. Who believed in what they were doing—believed themselves to be important. She'd taken the first job she'd been offered, convinced that without graduating she wouldn't be able to get anything else. And then she had stayed for years as it had gradually eaten away her ambition and her passion. It was like a light being switched on, being here at Finn's company. And he had offered her the way out.

Not a job that she hadn't earned, but something more fundamental than that. He had given her the chance to go back and pick up where she had left off. To retrace her steps back to the moment that her life had taken a catastrophic swerve and try to correct its course.

She got to decide now, what she wanted from her life, how she was going to define herself, and it was Finn who was offering her that chance.

Why? Why did he care so much? Yes, there was that chemistry between them— so much more complicated and confusing than the desire that normally characterised her relationships. Men who wanted her for her body. Men she wanted for their shallowness, their inability to hurt her. What she had felt with Finn that night, when she had woken in the morning with her body wrapped around his, protected by his, that was a far cry from simple. It was anything but shallow.

She had been adamant that these feelings they were having were not welcome, and were certainly not going to be acted upon. But, even without that future, one that they both knew was impossible, she was in no doubt that Finn *saw* her. Not her body, but her. He'd recognised the passion, the yearning she felt for the career that she'd left behind. And more than just seeing, he'd talked to her about it. Given her chances and choices, if she wanted to take them.

She put her finger to her lips as she walked into the office, and Finn came to admire her top babysitting and the sleeping babies in the pushchair. Then he parked them just inside the door and gestured to the table where lunch had been laid out for them.

'Fancy,' she said with an impressed smile.

Finn shrugged. 'Perk of being the boss. No such thing as a free lunch, though. Do you mind if I pick your brains about CVs before the interviews?'

Madeleine grabbed a plate and a stack

of resumes and started reading, raising an eyebrow from time to time.

'This is…impressive,' she said as she read about languages spoken and subjects tutored. Cookery skills and forest school trips and school entry exams. 'Though I think this is a little high-achieving for a couple of kids who aren't yet crawling,' she said with a shrug. 'I mean, it's great that she offers all this, but where's the care for the kids' emotional well-being? She hasn't mentioned that once.'

She grabbed another CV from the pile and started to read. Then laid it on top of the first. With the third, she broke into a smile. 'This one,' she said simply. 'Josie. The love she had for her last family totally shines through.'

Finn smiled. Josie had been top of his list too, and was lined up first for the interviews. Though why it should make him so happy that he and Madeleine agreed on this was anyone's guess. Oh, for God's sake, who was he trying to kid? He knew exactly why he was pleased that they saw eye to eye on this decision, and he knew exactly why he should be shutting down any thoughts that pointed in that dangerous direction.

'Well, I guess we could give them all a fair shot,' he said, glancing at the clock. 'I'll get this cleared away and have them send the first one through. Make sure you have coffee. These things can be gruelling.'

He was on his fourth cup of the day and it was doing nothing to keep his yawns at bay. The babies hadn't given him any trouble the night before, but he had lain awake regardless, desperately trying not to remember how it had felt to wake up Sunday morning with Madeleine practically in his lap. Saturday night had been long, and thankless. But then, right at the end, a kind of perfect.

He shook his head. Perfect. Except it never could be with her. He'd proved with Caro that he couldn't hold a marriage together. And failing again? Losing his home again? Compromising his business again? Never going to happen. He could feel the burn of bile in his throat at just the thought of it.

He couldn't afford to fail. Couldn't afford to lose any other part of the life that he'd built for himself. Everything up to this point had been about momentum. One success after another had changed his life beyond recognition. Losing Caro, his home—that had been his first failure and it had hit him hard. Hard enough to have learnt his lesson that he couldn't have both a relationship and his life. There was no way that he was starting something with Madeleine just to prove to himself that it really wasn't possible.

The stakes were too high to take that kind of risk. He had thought it bad enough when his marriage had broken down and he'd had to keep his life and his business on track. If he had let one more thing drop, he could have lost everything. If he had taken his eye off the ball once in the last year, when he was putting his life back together, it could all have been gone.

Now he had Bella and Hart to think about, the stakes were higher than they had ever been before. The dangers of failing were worse than ever. He wasn't going to ever let them be in the situation he had faced as a child. And that meant protecting what he had now. Much as he had strong feelings for Madeleine, he couldn't risk anything that would disrupt the careful equilibrium that he had managed to re-establish in the wake of his marriage failing. And if the only way to avoid that was to turn his back on this thing that was developing with Madeleine, then he'd do it, no matter how much it hurt, because the alternative was all too terrifying.

It would be easier, he supposed, if he could cut her out of his life completely. But he had promised Jake this favour. No. It wasn't about what he had promised Jake; it was about supporting Madeleine because it was the right thing to do and because he wanted to. He just had to draw that line between friendly support and falling asleep with her in his arms. How hard could that be?

Josie arrived—the nanny candidate who had topped both his and Madeleine's list— and he turned his attention to finding the best possible person to help care for his children. This was the way to keep his life on track—by concentrating on what his children needed, what would make their lives richer. If he could push his own desires into some tiny space in his mind and ignore them then he would be all the happier for it.

Madeleine kept one eye on Finn's expression as he conducted the first of the interviews, and couldn't put her finger on what was going on in that brain of his. She could sense him withdrawing from her, and if she hadn't been so relieved that he was fighting this as hard as she was then she would have been hurt.

Maybe it was just the business setting, but any closeness that had been there on Saturday night was well and truly gone by the time that the first interview was over. The twins woke up just in time to have a play with Josie, and as she and Finn took them over to their sensory cupboard Madeleine leaned back in her seat and watched them together. The nanny was perfect, and Madeleine felt a little sorry for the other candidates who were going to have to try and follow her this afternoon.

They're a perfect unit, Madeleine thought. And this was what she would be leaving behind when she made a decision about what to do with her life. Finn was already making plans, and she needed to too. Tonight, she promised herself. Tonight she was going to sit down with her laptop and make a real plan.

'Would you walk down with me, Madeleine?' Josie asked, tucking her braids behind her ear, and Madeleine's eyes widened with surprise. She'd asked Josie a couple of questions in the interview, but she had wanted to give Josie and Finn and the kids some time to get to know each other without a practical stranger there making things awkward. She lifted an eyebrow in question at Finn, who just smiled and tickled Bella under the chin.

'Fine with me,' he said, smiling as Bella laughed.

Madeleine shrugged and Finn followed her and Josie to the door. 'Thanks so much for coming in,' he said with genuine warmth. 'I'll be in touch in a couple of days. If you have any questions in the meantime, just send them over.'

'Great,' Josie said with a final smile. 'I'll look forward to hearing from you then.'

'So,' Madeleine said as they crossed to the lift and waited, 'was there something you wanted to ask?'

Josie hesitated until the lift arrived and, once she was inside, said, 'I just wanted to ask how it is living with Finn? I've had some live-in jobs that were better than others, you know. Finn seems great and Hart and Bella are adorable. I just wanted to sound you out—woman to woman—if there's anything else I should know about living with them.'

Ah, the penny dropped. Madeleine didn't need to imagine the awkward situations a live-in nanny could face. Add a single dad into the situation and she should totally understand her asking the question.

She thought back to her first night at Finn's, when she'd misunderstood his intentions. When he'd done everything in his power to make sure she knew that she was safe.

'He's honestly a great guy,' she told Josie without a hint of hesitation. 'I wouldn't have any reservations telling you that you should totally take the job if he offers.'

Josie smiled and Madeleine saw her

shoulders relax a fraction. 'That's such good news. I hope I'll see you again,' she said with a smile.

Madeleine waved her off and returned to the lifts feeling pensive. Well, looked like Josie had found her dream job. Finn had his domestic crisis sorted. She was the only one now who had to get her life in order.

She heard Finn speaking as she approached his office and hesitated in the doorway. He spotted her and gestured for her to wait—it was only then that she realised who he was speaking to. She recognised Caro from her voice, and from the way that Finn was angling the phone, showing the screen to two giggling babies; it was clear that they were video calling again.

'You'll Skype me into the second-round interview?' she heard Caro say as Finn began to wrap up the call.

Madeleine concentrated on repacking the twins' changing bag, trying not to eavesdrop on Finn's conversation with his wife. Ex-wife.

From the way the interview had gone, and the tone of Caroline's voice, Josie was probably going to be receiving a job offer pretty soon, and that meant that she had to work out a plan for what she was going to do next. Once Finn had a nanny in place, he wasn't going to want her living in his spare room. She'd known ever since she'd been made redundant that she was going to have to make big decisions, and her thinking time was almost up. If she didn't act now, she was going to find herself running out of options.

Since she'd walked out on her university education, she'd gone from one precariously held flat to another. The only constant—the job that she despised—even that was gone now. She had nothing to show for her life, and nothing made that more clear than being in Finn's office with his successful business and adorable children and his grown-up co-parenting.

So she had to think about Finn's offer. Had to think seriously about whether university was what she still wanted. Whether journalism and politics were what she still wanted. Because, for the first time in forever, she could actually choose what she *wanted*. Not what options were left to her. Not what she could afford, or which seemed to throw the least hurdles in her way. She had been given permission by the universe to make a fresh start. To be whatever she chose.

Was Finn one of those options? They had both been upfront about the fact that they didn't want a relationship. God knew he had told her that enough times. Roughly the same number of times that she had said the same thing. But… But did she mean it? Definitely the first time she had said it, and the second. But she had been less and less convinced by her own internal monologue as the days had gone on.

More importantly, he'd made her see that no one was putting more restrictions on her life than herself. Now was the time in her life she could make a change.

Finn had told her that he would help her financially. If she was turning him down because of—what?—some need to do this without his help?—who was she hurting? Only herself. It didn't make any difference to Finn or to anyone else in the world if she didn't go back to university. The only person it affected was herself.

Didn't she owe herself another chance? What else had she worked so hard for all those years? It didn't matter how resolutely she'd tried to ignore her dreams, to pretend that they meant nothing to her, they weren't going anywhere. Finn had seen them. He'd made her see them again too. To look at them straight on in a way that she'd been afraid to do for years. He thought they were worth fighting for. What did it say that he had read them so plainly on her face?

It said something unsettling. Unnerving. That she was so easy to read. Or maybe that Finn could read her easily—that wasn't the same thing at all, and she knew which one was true. Finn understood her. He *saw* her. And she wasn't sure where that left any consideration on her part about accepting money from him.

He hung up the phone and she crossed to the stack of CVs that they had left on his desk to remind herself of the next candidate. But the words swam in front of her eyes as she considered her next move. If Finn was serious about funding her, she had so many options that it was dizzying. Once, years ago, she'd looked briefly at the costs of going back to her studies and it had been beyond anything that she could dream of. Even a distance learning course would have left her hopelessly broke. But if she got a loan from Finn to cover her living costs, a student loan would cover her fees. She needn't be entirely dependent on Finn. If she was going to take this seriously, she could apply for some of the grants and bursaries and scholarships that had been so overwhelming when she had looked before. If she really wanted to do this, she could start applying for them now, and do it all by herself.

When the knock on the door snapped her back into the room, Finn had a half-smile on his face that she didn't have to work hard to interpret. She knew that her excitement was showing on her face, knew that Finn knew her well enough to guess what was going through her mind. But she wasn't going to share. Not yet, when it was still so fresh and delicate and unformed in her mind. She'd share later, when she was ready, and she knew Finn wasn't going to rush her.

And at that thought she was hit by a

wave of desire for him that stole her breath and made her look away for fear that he was going to see exactly what swerve her thoughts had just taken. Because these feelings that she was having for Finn weren't just a case of lusting after a pretty face. He'd had that face for years and she'd barely noticed it. It was about seeing the man he'd become—capable, successful, generous, kind—and desperately wanting to keep him in her life. And yes, the pretty face made these thoughts extra lusty, but the wanting wasn't about the face or the body. It was about nurturing this connection. This feeling of seeing and being seen. About taking care of someone she absolutely knew would take care of her.

And those feelings were huge and hot and terrifying—and absolutely undeniable. Now that she saw the truth of them, it was hard to believe that she'd ever been able to ignore them. They'd burst to life outside his bedroom door the first night that she'd spent in his home, when he'd seen her vulnerability and stood by her side as she'd found her strength, and she'd been kidding herself ever since that these feelings were something she could 'manage'.

These damn inconvenient feelings were about as far from manageable as she could imagine. But at least they were both agreed that they weren't happy about them. Right now, the fact that Finn was fighting them as hard as she was was just about the only thing stopping her doing something really stupid.

The knock on the door from Finn's assistant stopped that train of thought heading somewhere that would get them into trouble and she pasted on a professional smile as the next candidate was shown into the room.

CHAPTER ELEVEN

THANK GOODNESS THE babies have gone down with barely a peep, Madeleine thought as she sat at the writing desk in her room and opened her laptop.

It had taken all her considerable will-power to get through the afternoon without a cheeky search on her phone to look at what loans and scholarships and grants were available for mature students. Now, with the kids asleep, she had all evening to research and start to come up with a plan.

An hour later she had a list of politics and journalism courses in London, application details for her shortlist, and every scholarship, grant and bursary that she could hunt down.

The next job would be finding somewhere to live. She had no idea how she would pay for a place yet, not until she'd found some sort of work, but she had to start trying to find somewhere. If she got into university, she could maybe get a place in a hall of residence but that would be months away, if she even managed to make it happen at all. And she didn't have months. She needed somewhere soon. She pulled up a flatmates website to see what was available, and how much money she was going to have to come up with to survive the next few months. Maybe she would be able to find some freelance work just to keep her going until she had this university thing sorted. A house share might not need the same financial information and upfront deposits as renting a place on her own. It wasn't ideal, but she wasn't sure what else she could do right now.

She looked up at a knock on the doorframe to see Finn standing there watching her.

'Just wondered if you fancy dinner?' he asked, and she realised that she was starving. 'What are you working on?' he said and she turned the laptop to show him, then frowned at the expression on his face.

'What?' she asked.

'I didn't realise you were looking for somewhere else already.'

'Of course I'm looking. It's great of you to let me stay but it was always the plan to find somewhere as soon as I could. Josie is great, so it seemed like you wouldn't need my help much longer.'

'That doesn't mean you have to move out.'

'I'm staying here to help you with the babies, Finn. If you have a nanny, then what would I be doing? It would be…weird.'

'You could stay as Jake's sister. As a friend.'

'I think we both know that it wouldn't be a good idea, Finn.'

'Why not?'

Why not?

He knew exactly why not.

Which meant that he was asking the question because he wanted her to say the answer out loud. Well, fine, if he wanted to be reckless then so be it.

'Because you like me, Finn. We both know it. The same way we both know that I like you. And if we stay here together under this roof much longer then one of us is going to do something that we regret. Saturday night already went too far.'

'Saturday night was nothing,' he said, though the expression on his face proved that it was a lie.

'Well, it didn't feel like nothing at the time. It didn't for me and I don't think it did for you either, no matter what you're trying to tell yourself today. If it was nothing, then neither of us would be thinking about it, and I know I am.' In fact, she wished she'd had a minute today when she wasn't thinking about it. When her mind wasn't drifting back to the feel of him wrapped around her. It was way too distracting. 'I think the best thing for everyone is for me to find somewhere to stay and remove the temptation for both of us.'

'You've no money; how are you going to find somewhere to rent?'

'Wow.' She stood up, planting her hands on her hips. If he wanted a fight about this then she was game. 'Thanks for that reality check, Finn. It actually hadn't occurred to me that I'm broke and screwed. Thank heavens you're here to remind me. Nice swerve on the subject, by the way. Don't think I didn't notice.'

Finn walked over and leaned against her desk, and she took a step away from him sharply; she was cross and the last thing she needed was him getting close and distracting her. Finn took a step back too, and she hated that he could read her so well.

'Sorry. I'm sorry. I didn't mean to be rude,' he said, looking genuinely conciliatory.

She rolled her eyes and didn't even care that it made her look like the stroppy teenager she was sure he must remember. 'I'm just excited,' she said. 'Getting ahead of myself, I guess, looking at courses and student loans and bursaries. I want it to happen now.'

'Don't apologise for being excited. I should be the one apologising. So you're thinking of going back to university?'

She smiled as she acknowledged to herself that she had already made the decision, and she wasn't going to change her mind.

'I'm going. I've been looking at courses, loans, scholarships. I'm sure I can do it. I just need to come up with a proper plan.'

'I've already said that I'll lend you the money,' he reminded her.

'And I've thanked you, and told you that I wouldn't feel comfortable taking it. I want to do this myself. I got myself here. I'm going to get myself out.'

Finn frowned, reached out to brush a hand against her arm. 'You *didn't* get your-self here, though, Madeleine. Someone did something terrible to you. That's why you're in this situation and I don't under-stand why you won't let me help you out of it.' He frowned at her, but she shook off his judgement. He didn't understand what it was like to be in her position.

'Because it's uncomfortable for me, Finn,' she told him. 'Because these feel-ings that I have for you are uncomfortable, and the thought of owing you thousands of pounds makes me feel sick.'

Finn shook his head. 'But you wouldn't owe it. I wouldn't expect you to pay me back.'

'Don't you see that makes it worse?' She sat heavily on the edge of the bed. 'Because then it would always be weird and I would never have the chance to make things equal between us.' She stood up again, needing to do something with her body to get rid of this fizz of anxious energy. Finn crossed his arms and held her gaze, not backing down for a second.

'You're making a big deal out of this when you really don't have to.' Finn perched on the edge of her desk, crossing his arms as he watched her pacing. 'It's just money. It doesn't make us unequal—you can take it without it meaning anything.'

'I just can't, Finn.' She shook her head. 'I need you to leave this now,' she said. She had made her decision, and nothing he could say would change her mind.

He rubbed a hand on his jaw and shook his head. 'Fine. I'll leave it. But I'm not going to pretend to be happy about it, Madeleine. It doesn't seem fair that I can owe you, but you can't owe me.'

She rolled her eyes. This again. 'I told you, you don't owe me anything, Finn. It was my parents, and Jake, who were generous. I didn't do anything. Anyway. We've talked this subject to death. If you want to help me talk through my ideas and come up with a plan, that would be great. If you're going to bulldoze over my wishes and continue to in-sist on your own way then we're going to fall out. Now, let's change the subject.'

He looked as if he was going to go for one last argument, but then changed his mind. 'Fine. Dinner?' he asked.

'Yes. I'm starving. I can cook or...'

'Trudy left something for us in the fridge. We just need to heat it up. Do you want to eat together or—'

'Of course we can eat together, Finn. I'm not planning on hiding in here. All of this is meant to be keeping us friends. I don't want things to be awkward. I'm pretty sure we can still manage to eat a meal together without things imploding.'

'Good. Then I'll see you downstairs in ten?'

'I'll see you there.'

Finn checked the time on his phone again as he glanced towards the stairs. He was sure that once Madeleine was down here and they were talking again this anxious feeling would go. But right now, waiting for her to come down from her bedroom, he could feel his whole body on the verge of a twitch.

She was moving out. Of course she was. She had never really moved in because this was only ever a temporary arrangement. But seeing her browsing that site looking for flatmates—that had struck him in a surprisingly painful way. And he didn't want to have to think about why it hurt. He just wanted to convince Madeleine that she didn't have to rush into anything and leave in a hurry. He hadn't even definitely decided if he was offering Josie a job. He couldn't, not until Caro had spoken to her too. Madeleine was totally jumping the gun. She could stay as long as she needed.

Which meant this probably wasn't about him hiring Josie at all. This was about the other thing that she'd said. The words that had made his stomach twist in anticipation. *We both know that I like you.* He'd goaded her into saying it—he wasn't stupid, he could see that. But he'd expected her to bring up what they'd said before. About chemistry. He hadn't expected her to come right out and just tell him that she liked him. He hated that just hearing those words had fired his blood and it was now making it difficult to sit still. It was all so schoolboy.

But the words had hit him hard and he wanted to know more. He would die before asking if she *liked him* liked him. But he was desperate to know if she was thinking of him as often as he was thinking of her. If daydreams and fantasies made it as impossible for her to concentrate as it did for him.

He looked up at a sound in the doorway and was arrested by the sight of her in his home. How had this happened? How had he found himself so undone by someone he had known for twenty years? Someone who until a few days ago had been a distant presence in his life. Someone he might kiss on the cheek at family parties but who otherwise didn't have a place in his life at all. Until she'd moved into his apartment and his brain and hadn't allowed him a minute's respite ever since.

'You like me?' he said, and as the words left his mouth he knew how dangerous a move that was. He knew that one of them, or both of them, were going to end up getting hurt because he had no way of following this conversation through. Of taking this friendship to another level—taking it to where he really wanted it to go. He couldn't risk a relationship. Couldn't risk his life falling apart when he had so narrowly averted that disaster. He had lost his home once. He wasn't taking his chances by making the same mistakes all over again.

Why was he even thinking about his divorce? He pulled himself up. No one had mentioned marriage. A relationship even. All Madeleine had done was tell him that she liked him and he was the one who had jumped all the way to the altar. It didn't have to be that way. There was a middle ground between a kiss on the cheek and marriage—and it would never be enough for him, he realised. Watching her watching him, he was convinced that nothing would ever be enough where Madeleine was concerned.

He had never wanted like this. Even in those early days with Caro when he had been so sure that he was in love, what he had really felt was relief and gratitude and comfort, he realised now—that he had someone who had been born into the world of CEOs and OBEs that he had suddenly found himself trying to navigate. Someone who knew how to move in that world and stop him feeling like the poor kid eating at someone else's table.

He could never escape that kid when he was with Madeleine. She saw him every time that she looked at him. And he didn't mind, he realised with a jolt. That kid was a part of his story. He was a part of Madeleine's story too. They both accepted that he had a place at their table. No point in either of them pretending that he didn't exist.

Madeleine had held his gaze this whole time, watching him while he grappled with how big a mistake he had made when he'd asked her that question. He loved watching her think. Loved watching her grapple with herself, deciding exactly how much of herself she wanted to reveal, how brave she wanted to be. She always took the brave option. He knew that she would.

'I like you,' she said.

She shrugged, as if the words were nothing more than a bland observation. They both knew they were so much more than that.

'Don't move out.'

Her eyebrows pinched together at his impulsive words, and he couldn't blame her.

Asking her to stay didn't make any sense. They both knew that the safest thing for them both to do right now was to keep their distance from one another. And yet here they both were. Alone in his house, eyes locked and guards tumbling.

'Why?'

She was calling his bluff, just as he'd called hers. And she'd already set the bar with her bravery and her honesty. He wasn't going to let her down by doing anything less.

'Because I like having you here.'

'You don't have me.'

Again, that pinch in her brow. He half smiled at the innuendo, wondering which of them was going to rein this flirting in. Not him. Not this time. Not yet.

'Maybe I would, if you stayed.'

She crossed her arms and leaned against the doorframe, her eyes never leaving his.

'That would be a terrible idea,' she said. And the words would have felt like a shot of ice water if it hadn't been for the expression in her eyes. The one that told him she cared about it being a bad idea about as much as he did right now.

That was fire. Not ice. He didn't want to be smart. He wanted to be stupid, if stupid meant wrapping his arms around Madeleine or rubbing that crease from her forehead with his thumb and making her forget her demons for a while. If stupid meant that his hands got to circle that little bone on her ankle again but explore further this time. Up long calves and soft thighs. If his arms could circle her waist as he pulled her under him.

'I agree,' he said at last. 'It's a terrible idea. But I can't stop thinking that I want to do it anyway. And I think you feel the same way.'

'Just because we're both thinking the same stupid thing doesn't mean we should act on it,' Madeleine observed with a lift of her eyebrow.

He left his stool and walked over to stand in front of her, his hands in his pockets as she looked him up and down. God, he would die happy if she just looked at him like that one more time.

'Agreed,' he said with a half-smile. 'Want to do it anyway?'

The moan she let out hit him straight in the gut and he was hard even before she took that step towards him, wrapped her arms around his neck until she was all he could see and hear and smell.

'A really bad idea,' she said again, but the smile on her lips—God, her lips…so close…so full…so pink—told him she was past brave. She'd headed straight through courage to reckless and he was right there with her.

There was no hesitation when her mouth finally met his. She pressed firm against him, her lips tasting and exploring, while he was so overwhelmed that this was happening that he barely knew how to respond. It was only when she broke the kiss and looked up at him, that little crease back on her brow, that he snapped back into the present, stopped overthinking and realised that he had everything he had been dreaming about right in front of him. In his next heartbeat his arms were around her waist, he had pulled her into his body and crashed them both back against the doorframe, her body soft in his arms, her breath in his mouth.

CHAPTER TWELVE

FINN CREPT BACK into his bedroom after settling Bella back to sleep and paused to take in the sight of Madeleine Everleigh asleep in his bed. The sheets were tucked across her chest, her head turned to one side and her hair messy around her on the pillows. In the half-light, he still couldn't quite believe what they'd done. That she'd wanted him as much as he realised he'd been yearning for her these past days. But now the spell was broken and he was out of bed—where did they go from here?

Could he just slip back into bed, wrap his arms around her and pretend the spell had never been broken? Or did he accept that his alarm was going off in an hour anyway and he might as well be up for the day? That must be the sensible thing to do. Because when he was too close to her he lost his mind. That was the only explanation for what had happened last night, when they had both jumped headfirst into something that they'd both said—out loud and on numerous occasions—was a very bad idea. And now they both knew exactly what they would be missing out on, he wasn't sure how they were ever meant to make a sensible decision again.

Nothing had changed for them. The fundamentals of their lives remained the same. He couldn't start a relationship now, couldn't add that layer of complication to a life that he had kept on track by the skin of his teeth. But…but last night. He had never felt so connected to another person. Which was a bad thing, he reminded himself for the thousandth time. Because neither he nor Madeleine wanted this to happen. So when the sun came up they would go back to being so very sensible and not letting this happen again. Wouldn't they?

Suddenly he wasn't so sure that that was what he wanted—to give up on the idea of ever having a relationship. But there really couldn't be a worse time. He had dragged himself out of poverty. He had worked every hour for a decade to build this business up. He had made the sort of marriage he had thought that he needed to survive in that world. And he'd tried his hardest to love her.

And all of that had nearly been derailed when his best hadn't been good enough and he and Caro had had to find a way to unpick their lives and their finances. He had lost his home. He couldn't face that sort of instability again—not now he had the twins. If the idea of losing everything he had worked for had been frightening before he had become a father, it was unthinkable now.

And yet…it wasn't quite morning. The babies were asleep and there was still an hour before his alarm would go off. If last night was all they were going to have then he wasn't going to waste the final hour of it examining his conscience.

He slipped back beneath the cool sheets and reached for Madeleine, an arm sliding under her waist, pulling her back towards him until he could feel the heat of her skin from his chest to his toes. She let out a huff of breath and tangled her fingers in his, pulling his arm tighter around her waist.

'Mmm...' she said, barely more than a whisper. 'Don't tell me it's morning.' He pressed a kiss to the nape of her neck, sweeping her hair out of the way to follow that thought around to her ear, her jaw.

'We've an hour until the alarm,' he said, fingers now exploring the soft skin of her belly, the dip of her waist, the ample curve of her hip. 'Want to go back to sleep?' He could feel her smile, even with her back to him, as she pressed herself just a tiny bit closer.

'Not even for a second.'

By the time his alarm sounded he was boneless and heavy, his eyes sore from lack of sleep, his body deliciously fatigued. As he reached to silence his phone, Madeleine shifted from where her head had been resting on his chest to look up at him.

'What are the chances we can ignore that and go back to sleep?'

He smiled at her and kissed her softly on the lips.

'You know I wish I could, but I have to go into the office. Will you be okay with the twins here for a couple of hours, or we could all go in together?'

'No, it's fine, we'll hang out here. I'm sure you've got lots to catch up on,' Madeleine said, pulling the sheet a little tighter around her. And like that it was over. Neither of them had even left the bed yet, but whatever it was that had allowed them to ignore their better judgement was gone, leaving awkwardness in its wake.

He caught her gaze and looked her in the eye, and was unreasonably pleased that she cracked him a half-smile. 'Are we okay?' he asked.

'Go to work,' she said. 'And stop worrying. We're fine, and if we need to talk we can do it later.'

If they needed to talk? On what planet did you sleep with your brother's best friend— the same person who also happened to be your temporary housemate and whose kids you were babysitting—and not need to talk about it? Maybe Finn would get home from work tonight and Trudy would have left dinner and they could just eat and put the babies to bed and not mention the fact that he'd made her see stars last night. Well, that was a perfectly reasonable plan, wasn't it?

She rolled her eyes at her own idiocy as she heard the shower in Finn's bathroom turn on and started to look around her and work out what had happened to her clothes. One minute they had been in the kitchen— all meaningful looks and barely concealed lust—and the next they were done with even barely concealing and they were crashing against doorframes and knocking into bannisters, shedding clothes as they went.

From here she could spot underwear, but she was going to have to grab Finn's shirt if she was going to make it out of here with any sort of dignity intact. Really, this whole morning-after thing would be so much easier if they had actually talked for even a second about how they were going to handle this today... They should just be going back to normal, right? Pretending that it had meant nothing and that they were little more than acquaintances to one another. Acquaintances who had seen one another naked and done any number of things that were making her blush now that she was thinking of them in the daylight.

But it wasn't going to go any further than that because…because what? Because this wasn't her style, getting involved with someone who she actually liked and respected. Because he was someone she could have a proper conversation with, someone she could rely on. Because he wasn't one of the shallow boys that she normally picked up and put down. Because she knew deep down that he saw her for who she really was. He was someone who supported and respected her.

Yeah, she told herself with a heavy touch of sarcasm. Why would she choose *that* for herself, when she had her life of meaningless, pointless dating to go back to? It wasn't as if the guy was a genius in bed or anything…

The shower stopped as she finished buttoning her shirt—his shirt—and for a moment she considered darting back into her own room. But that would be idiotic, she told herself. She'd got herself here—into this room, this situation—and she could get herself out of it with at least a little dignity intact.

'Hey, you didn't have to get up,' Finn

said as he walked back into the room and clocked her standing beside the bed in his shirt. 'Looks good on you,' he said with a smirk that was one hundred per cent alpha male marking his territory. In a really good way.

On her way back to her own room she could hear Hart stirring in his cot and decided to go in before he could wake up his sister. Carrying him down towards the kitchen, she sniffed the top of his head and asked herself for the thousandth time what she was going to do next. Everything that had happened last night had stemmed from a conversation about making plans for her future—and instead of finding an answer to that conundrum, all she had done was make the status quo even more awkward— had possibly even tipped it over into untenable. As soon as she had had enough coffee—eight or so espressos should probably do the trick—she would fetch her laptop down from her room and resume her search for somewhere to live.

Her employers had promised her pay in lieu of the statutory notice period, as well as the redundancy pay she was legally entitled to, but so far her bank balance wasn't showing any sign of their making good on this. Great. She could get the money she was legally owed if she pursued it through the courts, of course, but that didn't help her a whole lot right this minute. And it would also suck up a lot of the time she had earmarked for university research. She didn't want to give that time to her crappy old company, along with everything else they'd taken from her.

She picked up items of discarded clothing, glad that Finn was still upstairs and therefore unable to see the fierce pink staining her cheeks. It was only when he appeared in the doorway, reversing their positions from the night before, that she remembered that she was still wearing his shirt—and very little else. Well, it was a bit late to be coy. There was no part of her—literally, she thought, not a single part of her—that he hadn't seen last night. Surely that should make her less embarrassed rather than more. But her cheeks were still glowing and there was no point trying to pretend that Finn couldn't see it. She handed him one of the coffees she'd made and started prepping bottles for Bella and Hart, anything to avoid eye contact or awkward conversation.

'That was great,' Finn said after hastily downing his coffee. 'You have my mobile and my office number, so if you're at all worried about the twins then give me a call, yes? I'll jump straight in the car if you need me back.'

She gave what she hoped was a neutral smile. 'We'll be absolutely fine. Now go to work.'

Finn paused before walking past her, and she knew he was making the same calculation as she was. Did they kiss on the cheek? On the lips? After all the places he'd kissed her just hours ago it seemed ridiculous that they could be paralysed by such a question now. But here they both were, with their rictus grins stretching wide, quite incapable of passing one another in the kitchen like normal adults.

Eventually Finn broke—he was the one who had to leave the house after all—and gave her a hasty peck on the cheek as he passed her on the way to the door. *Fine— no eye contact, don't turn back*. Determined not to lift her fingers to the spot where the impression of his lips was still burning her already pink cheeks.

It was only when she heard the front door close that she allowed herself to unstick her feet from the floor and resume normal movement, moving around the kitchen until she had a plate of toast in front of her and Hart was drinking enthusiastically from a bottle. And then somehow it was nearly lunchtime, and the morning had disappeared in another round of milk-feeding and nappy-changing and pram-rocking.

Finally, in an attempt to buy herself enough time to sit down with a hot drink, she loaded both babies—sleepy and well-fed and clean and dry—into the double pushchair and determined just to keep walking until they both gave in and had a nap.

The leafy streets and quiet gardens around Finn's townhouse were hardly a trial to kill an hour in, and she had an entertaining time trying to peer into expensively shuttered and curtained bay windows, spotting grand pianos and silk chaises longues, sleek kitchens and surprised-looking neighbours. By the time that she had done her third lap around the block with the delicious-looking patisserie on the corner, both Hart and Bella had succumbed to the motion of the pram and were peacefully asleep.

Sighing with relief at the sight of a free outdoor table, Madeleine parked the twins in the shade and pulled out her phone. She could have a coffee and get a spot of research done, and all before lunch. Really, she was better at this babysitting lark than she had thought. It was hard to consider this as anything other than gloriously successful.

She pulled up her online banking app and tapped in her passcode. She had been avoiding looking at it for the past few days, not keen on having a concrete reminder of exactly how dire things really were. But if she was going to find somewhere to stay, she couldn't hide from the ugly truth for ever.

She squinted as the balance loaded, trying to brace herself against the flash of panic that was her norm in this situation. But the number on the screen was so far from what she was expecting that her eyes widened involuntarily. Had her former employers actually come good on their promise of redundancy pay, and pay in lieu of notice and—what?—a year's back pay that she had somehow not realised she was owed?

She clicked through to her recent transactions, to find the unfeasibly large deposit in her current account. This just didn't make sense. How had they even found the cash to pay her this much? And then she saw the name associated with the deposit.

He hadn't…

Oh, my God.

If he had done this, she was never going to talk to him again. She was going to kill him. She was going to kill him and then never talk to him again, which would be considerably easier once he was six feet under.

And then through her anger came a crashing wave of shame. Heat that started in her cheeks before spreading to her chest, down her arms, until it felt as if her whole body was burning with it. Was that what he thought of her? That she would accept money from him after last night? Had he thought that she was expecting it? Had she done something to make him think that that was who she was—so mercenary? So grasping.

She picked up her phone to give him an earful but stopped herself before she dialled. She didn't want to do this in a rage, so emotional. She wanted him to see her ice cool and totally in control. By the time he got back that night she could be packed. Jake would put her up for a night or shout her a stay in a cheap hotel. She didn't have it all worked out yet, but she was absolutely certain that she wasn't spending another night under Finn's roof, and she wasn't touching a penny of that money. As the flush began to fade, her skin began to crawl as every moment from the night before was cast in a new light—one where Finn was planning on paying for the pleasure.

CHAPTER THIRTEEN

FINN HESITATED AT the door as he dug out his keys, wondering what he was going to find inside. His texts to Madeleine had garnered *We're all fine* as a response. Which was… fine. But at the same time the brusqueness of those three words made him nervous. If he had thought that finally sleeping with Madeleine would make it easier to concentrate on his work, then he couldn't have been more wrong. He'd thought about nothing but her all day. Through various meetings that really should have had his full attention. During the lunch that he'd grabbed at his desk. In the car on the way home.

All seemed quiet, he noted as he turned his key in the lock and opened the door. From the hallway he followed the sound of babies laughing right up the stairs until he found Bella, Hart and Madeleine all lying on the play mat in the nursery, staring up at the stars projected on the ceiling. The babies were in pyjamas, looking freshly bathed and content, and there were two empty bottles on the dresser beside the glider chair. He'd tried to get home for their bedtime, but had been waylaid on his way out and was back half an hour after they'd usually be asleep. But Madeleine had known, it seemed, that he'd want to say goodnight to them. His heart throbbed at her understanding that. And then he saw her spot him standing by the door.

She sat straight up and the playful look on her face was replaced immediately with pure fury. He took a reflexive step back as she walked towards him and scrambled to keep up with the abrupt change of atmosphere.

'They're ready to go to sleep,' she all but hissed at him as she approached the door. 'Hart will go sooner than Bella, I think. Trudy left dinner in the oven.'

He frowned as he watched her walk down the corridor, grab a bag from her room and head for the stairs. 'Wait!' he called, jogging after her. 'What's going on, Madeleine? I know things are a bit awkward after last night, but you don't have to—'

'A bit awkward? *A bit awkward?*' Madeleine whisper-shouted, anger radiating. 'This morning in the kitchen was *a bit awkward*, Finn. Now…now we are so far past awkward that I actually kind of miss it. We left it behind when you decided to pay me for my services.'

'Services? I don't know what—'

And then he did know. Saw how it must have looked to Madeleine and wanted to bang his head against the nearest wall to knock the stupidity out.

He'd deposited thousands of pounds into her bank account the morning after they had slept together. Of course it didn't look great. But that wasn't what he had meant by it—not at all, but it didn't look as if Madeleine was planning on sticking round long enough to hear him out on it. And how could he blame her for that?

'Oh, no, Madeleine. I see how it looks and I promise it's not like that. Not at all. I just wanted to help and you were so excited about university and this way you could be sure you had the finances in place. *Please*, please will you stick around until I've got the kids to sleep and we can talk about it properly?'

He couldn't do this in a stage whisper, waiting for a cry from the twins. He just needed her to wait one hour and they could sort all this out.

She glanced at her watch and then at the front door, and for a second he thought that he'd lost her. But she dropped the bag and his heart started beating again, a tattoo of relief.

'I'll wait in the kitchen until seven-thirty,' she said, glancing at her watch. 'But after that I'm going and I'm not coming back, Finn.'

'I'll be down before then, I promise you, and we will sort this out.'

Madeleine sat in the kitchen nursing a cup of tea and texting Jake while she waited for Finn to get the babies to sleep. She'd dropped him a text asking if she could stay the night, and he'd texted straight back asking what had happened with Finn. And so it begins, she thought. Suddenly she could see endless questions about 'What happened with Finn?' in her future and had no idea how to answer them.

And if she didn't tell, then Jake was only going to ask Finn, and she didn't even want to think about what he would tell her brother. Surely he wouldn't be so base as to tell him what had happened. But then before today she hadn't thought that he would chuck a big lump of cash in her bank account after they had spent the night together either. Turned out she didn't know Finn as well as she'd thought that she did.

Which shouldn't have been a surprise, really, considering that they had only spent a handful of days together since she had left her childhood home for university. But in those few days he had really convinced her that he understood her. That he knew her. She had told him things that she had never told anyone else. And he hadn't listened at all. Not really listened, not if he thought that he could treat her the way that he had today and that she would be fine with that.

She thought about the explanations that

he had given her: that he wanted her to have certainty about her university finances, as if she were some eighteen-year-old schoolgirl who needed someone to help her navigate the world of student loans, rather than a woman the other side of thirty who had been handling her overdraft for nearly half her life and was perfectly capable of finding a scholarship for herself.

He didn't think she could do it.

If the money wasn't payment for services rendered, then it was something else. It was a tacit acknowledgement that he didn't think that she would be able to do it by herself. He was rescuing her before she even needed it, so sure was he that she was going to fail. By the time that he walked into the room at seven twenty-five, she was halfway decided that she was just going to walk without hearing him out. What could he possibly say that would make up for his utter lack of faith in or respect for her?

'Madeleine, if you'll hear me out, I'd like to explain.'

'I don't think there's anything you can say, Finn,' she said, crossing her arms across her body and making it clear she was putting firm boundaries in place. As far as she was concerned, the intimacies of last night had never happened. 'I stayed because I didn't want to do this in front of the twins, and they needed to go to sleep. But you can't undo what you did, so I think it's best if I go. I'll return the money, of course. It's best if we keep out of each other's way for a while.'

He shook his head and came to lean on the kitchen island opposite her. She couldn't look him in the eyes, not if she wanted to remember that she was keeping her distance, emotionally as well as physically.

'You don't have to go,' he said. 'I realise now what it must look like, and I'm sorry. But I was always going to give you the money for university. It had nothing to do with last night.'

'It had nothing to do with what I actually wanted either,' Madeleine said, finding in her anger that she could look at him directly. 'I know you expect me to be grateful, but I didn't ask for your money. I didn't want it when you offered it to me. I can do this myself, and I have every intention of doing so.'

'But you don't need to,' he countered, looking genuinely confused that she might want to do this on her own. 'Why won't you accept a little help?'

'Why won't you accept that I don't need your help?' she said, sliding off her stool and standing opposite him. 'Yes, you did me a favour by letting me stay here, but I want to get back on my own feet. I've never wanted to be dependent on you. Not before last night, and definitely not after.'

He frowned at her, and she wondered if he was being dense on purpose. 'Would that be so awful, having to depend on another person?' Finn asked.

'Do you depend on anyone?' she asked. 'Do you look to someone else to pay your bills?' She planted her hands on her hips, trying to ground herself and stay rational. But he was so infuriating it was becoming an impossible task. 'No. You did it all yourself, but you don't believe that I can. If you believed in me, you wouldn't have to sneak money into my bank account like that.'

Finn threw his hands in the air, and she

could tell he was as frustrated as she was. 'Of course I believe that you can do it yourself. I just don't think you should have to. This way you can be certain that you've got a place to stay. I don't see why that's a bad thing.'

'I was sure that I could find another way. You're the only one who wasn't.'

'But why risk the uncertainty?' he asked, and she could hear his frustration in the strain of his voice. 'Why risk finding yourself with nowhere to live? Again.'

She talked low and slow, so he couldn't be in any doubt about how angry she was with him. 'I can risk it because I believe in myself. It's called confidence, Finn. Faith. Something you seem to be lacking in me.'

His hands had dropped to the countertop now, and he was leaning heavily on it.

'I don't think you understand. If something went wrong…'

'You don't think I understand? I turned up on your doorstep with nowhere else to go, with no job and no idea of what I was going to do next. And you think I don't understand? If something went wrong, I would try again,' she said, still speaking slowly. 'And I would keep trying until I'd done it. Isn't that how you got to where you are?'

'Yes, but...'

She paused, looked at him, at the way the colour had drained from his face.

'You've never failed, have you?' she said, realisation crashing over her. 'You've gone from one piece of good luck to another and never had to live with the consequences when it's all gone wrong.'

'Ha!' Finn said with a laugh that didn't sound at all genuine. 'You don't understand what you're talking about, Madeleine.'

'Sure I do. You're the head of a huge company, in beautiful new offices. You have two beautiful children and this gorgeous home. You've got everything that you ever wanted. You can't even imagine how I would survive if my plans didn't work out first time. I mean, look at everything you've achieved.' She watched him closely, trying to read his body language, his face. She had spilled more secrets to him than she'd ever thought she could, and now it was time to even the score.

'You don't know what you're talking

about,' he said again, his voice lower, more dangerous. 'You look around and see an apartment. I see failure. I see the house I should have been bringing my children up in, sold in the divorce because I couldn't make my marriage work. It was gone. I didn't even know—still don't know—how my marriage disintegrated so fast. And my home was gone, and the business holding on by a thread. And I could so easily have lost everything. I still could.'

'You're terrified,' she realised, looking at him, really seeing his life for the first time. Suddenly it all made sense. The drive, the ambition. 'You're terrified that all this is going to fail and you'll lose everything.' And he had been projecting all his worst fears onto her rather than face up to them. 'You're so afraid of failure that you can't bear the thought that my plans might not work out, so you pumped my bank account full of money to make sure that won't happen.'

'That's not it,' Finn said. But she could read his face. His heart wasn't even in the denial. That was *exactly* it.

'Why are you so scared?' she asked.

'You have this apartment. You have your business. You could walk away now a rich man.'

'I could, and then there could be another financial crisis and I could lose everything and the apartment would be gone and the kids... What would we do? I thought I was set for life. I thought the business was good and my home life was good and I thought I could see how the future was going to unfold. And then Caro told me that she was unhappy, that she was leaving, and it all fell away. I thought it was all secure, and it wasn't. Not a single part of my life made it out of the divorce unscathed. And I can't risk that again. I won't.'

And there it was. This was what he was really afraid of—finding himself a hungry little boy again. Seeing his children live the same childhood that he had. She was hit by a wave of sympathy, taking the edge off her anger.

'Your mother coped with worse,' she reminded him, 'and you turned out okay.' Because, really, the huge chunk of money she hadn't asked for aside, Finn was a decent guy and she knew his mother was proud of him.

'She did. She coped. Every single day she worked two jobs, sometimes more, to keep barely enough food in the cupboard for me, and she coped. And that's all she did. So that by the time that I had enough money for her not to have to work any more she was too worn out and tired to enjoy the benefits.'

'And you're frightened of ending up like her. I understand that. But you did it, Finn. You worked hard for her, and yourself, and you're a million miles away from that life now. You're not going to wake up one day and find yourself back there.'

'But what's the difference, really?' he asked, looking haunted. 'It's the figures in my bank accounts. It's not real money; it's just numbers. It's intangible. When Caro and I got divorced, that number halved. The house went. I nearly lost the business too. Anything could happen. The business could still fail. One of the kids could get sick. There are a million things waiting around the corner that will mean that all that work wasn't enough and I'll find myself back where I started. Where my mum started.'

'Your marriage ended and that meant you'd failed. That's what you think, right? You failed, putting everything at risk.' She so had him sussed, and he was wrong, and she was going to make him see it. Not for herself, she told herself, but as a service to her friend. She had no interest in whether he was relationship material or not, because she absolutely didn't want one herself. But she couldn't let him go on with his life scared to start a relationship because he was convinced that he was going to lose everything. That he wouldn't be able to cope if that happened. He was a good guy, and he deserved better than that.

'Well, we're divorced,' Finn said eventually. 'I don't think we can call it a roaring success of a marriage.'

She rested her elbows on the countertop, leaning towards him in a challenge. 'You could call it two people growing apart and making a positive decision for their future happiness.'

'*You* could call it that, if you wanted to.' Finn took a step backwards and she knew that her words had hit home. 'I just see it for what it was. Something that should have been better. Something that would have been better, if I'd worked a little harder.'

She laughed, only stopping herself when she saw the hurt on his face. 'You think your marriage ended because you didn't work hard enough?'

'That was part of it.' He nodded.

'And the other parts?'

'What do the other parts matter?' She was pressed up against the counter now and he had retreated to the other side of the room. He was on the run, but she was going to make him face up to this. He had put her in this position by putting that money into her account when she had specifically told him not to. She wasn't going to hold off making him as uncomfortable as he had made her.

'I imagine they mattered to Caro.' He was the one with his arms crossed now. She saw the barriers he had thrown up and ignored them. This was too important. 'Did you talk about it, when things started to go wrong?' she asked.

'Yes, of course, but by then it was too late.

We wanted different things: I wanted to be settled here and she wanted something... *more*.'

Madeleine shrugged. 'Doesn't sound like there's a lot you could have done about that.'

'I could have tried to go with her.'

'Was that what you wanted?'

He hesitated, looked thoughtful. 'No.'

'Then I can't imagine it would have made for a fulfilling arrangement for either of you. Sounds like the decision to end the marriage was a pretty successful one for both of you. So why did it feel so scary? Was it the money?'

He shook his head. 'We split things fifty-fifty. It was fair.'

'I'm sure it was. What aren't you telling me, Finn? I know there's more to this.'

His eyes snapped up to hers and she realised she'd been thinking out loud. He dropped his head into his hands before he answered, and pressed hard against his eyes. 'I lost my home, Maddie,' he said when he looked up. 'I waited so long to have my own home, with food always in the fridge. With the heating always on.

And I married Caro and we bought our house, and I thought that that was it. That I never had to worry again. And then— so quickly—it was all gone. Just…gone. And at the same time we were building the new business premises, and the numbers weren't adding up. And for the first time since I was a kid I was *scared*, Madeleine. I was scared that it wasn't all going to come good in the end. That I was going to find myself hungry. And cold. And back on Jake's doorstep, looking for someone to take me in. I couldn't bear that. I couldn't bear to lose everything that I had worked so hard for. For it all to come to nothing.'

She watched as he crossed to the fridge, grabbed a beer and slid a couple of slices of bread into the toaster, and wondered if it was conscious. That need to go and get the food that was always available now.

'No wonder you're not ready for this,' she said, and his eyes snapped to her. How could he be ready for a relationship when he was paralysed by his fear of what would happen if it all went wrong? Far safer to sabotage the whole thing before it even got off the ground. 'But, you know, just because things went wrong once before, that doesn't mean it would happen again. You lost an awful lot when Caro went, and I'm not talking about the money and the house. Or even your wife. I'm talking about feeling safe, and secure. And loved. But you survived it. And you have the twins and a lot to show for those years you were married. Would you rather you'd never met Caro? Never married her?'

She saw him think about it, and then the expression on his face softened. 'No. I wouldn't have the twins if I'd never met her. I wouldn't... Everything that has happened in my life has led me here. Tonight. And I'm not sure I can wish that away.'

When he shot her a particularly intense look she had to look away. It was *good* that he wasn't ready for this, she told herself. *She* wasn't ready for this. She didn't *want* this. Not with her new plans for her life buzzing and sparking in her brain. She didn't want to be distracted by a man. Least of all one who wouldn't give her the space or opportunity to make her own mistakes—forge her own path.

She wasn't ready for this. It wasn't that

she didn't want him. It wasn't that she didn't want a relationship, she realised. It was that she wasn't ready.

But that realisation made her wonder—did she *want* to be ready? Did she want *him* to be ready? She'd spent the last hour trying to make Finn see that his reasons for not wanting to ever have a new relationship didn't hold up to scrutiny. They were based on fear, not a choice. Were her reasons the same? For years she'd kept her relationships exactly how she wanted them: non-committal. Non-threatening. And they'd left her kind of…empty. If she wanted more out of a relationship, she was going to have to give more. And that scared the hell out of her.

Maybe she shouldn't be trying to help Finn. Maybe she should be leaving him with his illusions because that would be safer for her. With both of them running scared from a relationship, she was doubly safe. If she made Finn face up to his issues and put aside his fears, there was one of her defences gone. If doing that made her see that her own approach to relationships was making her unhappy and needed to change, then there was the second front defeated as well.

But somehow that seemed less important this evening than making Finn feel that he was safe. That he would still be safe if he decided to take a chance on a new relationship. That marriages ended and houses got sold and the world didn't fall in. He would never be as vulnerable as he was as a cold, hungry child again. And not because he was rich, right this minute. But because he was tough and worldly and had—as he always did—people who loved him, who had his back. She wanted him to know that he could take a chance on falling in love without fearing that he was putting his children at risk. That the fears that he had been carrying around didn't need to control his decisions or define his future. She would put her own fears aside for now, if it meant helping him.

Which was pretty much a one-eighty from the shouting match that she'd thought she was preparing for when she had found that money in her account. But it was so clear to her that the money had nothing to do with his faith in her abilities. She believed that he believed in her. His doubts were all in himself. She knew that she couldn't change that by herself, but she hoped that by pointing out what was so obvious to her, he would start to believe her.

'Why are you so invested in this?' Finn asked her and she had to admire the way that he was turning the conversation away from himself. It was what she wanted to do now—to take a swerve rather than face up to her own feelings. But she wanted him to be brave, and that meant that she had to be brave too, no matter the consequences. Wasn't that what they'd been doing with one another since she'd arrived? Being brave.

'Why do you think?' she said. 'Because I care about you. I think these fears are keeping you from being happy. I want you to be happy.'

'Because of what happened last night? Because you want more.'

She shook her head, smiling. 'You know that's not it, Finn. I said I didn't and I meant it.'

'I know that's what you said. Was it true? Is it still true now?'

She could turn this around on him again, if she wanted. She could be all *Do you want me to want you to want me?* and they could continue going round in circles all night. Or she could tell him what she was actually feeling and see if he was going to put himself out there with her.

'I don't know what I want. Before last night, if you'd asked me, I would have sworn that I want to keep things casual. That I don't want to get too involved. Not just with you. With anyone. Today... I'm not sure. I'm not sure that my reasons for keeping my distance in relationships are good ones. I need to think about that some more. Now, are you going to be honest and tell me what you're feeling too? Or am I out here on this ledge on my own?'

He came back across to the counter, leaned on it, their body language mirrored across this great hunk of granite.

Pretty pathetic that this is the closest I've been to someone for years, she thought to herself.

Yes, they had been physically closer last night—but this here was the real scary stuff.

'People fall off ledges all the time, you

know,' Finn said. 'Gravity is pretty unforgiving. They hurtle down and smash onto the ground below. Who walks into that situation willingly?'

She smiled at the metaphor because he was really throwing everything that he had at resisting what was starting to look pretty tempting to her.

'Everyone does, Finn. People do it every day. People pick themselves up after divorce, or harassment, or any number of other horrible situations, and they try again. Because what's the alternative?'

'Is that what you're doing?' he said, answering her question with a question. 'Trying again?'

She shrugged because at this point she honestly wasn't sure. 'I don't know. I'm thinking about it. But you're leaving me hanging here.'

'I care about you too.' Holy crap. He was tiptoeing out onto the ledge. 'You know that I care about you, Maddie. But I don't know how we decide to do this. That all the reasons—all the really good reasons—we have for not doing this don't matter any more.'

She thought about that for a second.

'Tell me what you think about my reasons then. Why do you think I've been fighting this?'

He smirked, and she knew how clearly he saw her. 'Because you like to be in control. Because someone took that from you once, and now you guard it with your life. Because you think that any man who shows you attention is only interested in one thing.'

She nodded, amazed that hearing those words coming from him could make her smile.

'Do you think I'm right?'

He stared at her longer than was comfortable. 'I think you have every reason to want to protect yourself.'

'But?' she prompted.

'But I think I've proven to you that not everyone who looks at you sees you that way. Some of us see *you*. And you deserve a chance. You deserve a chance to be happy.'

'So, to summarise, you think I should take a risk. But you're not prepared to take one with me?'

Oh, they were really doing this. Her heart started pounding and she could feel the heat in her cheeks as her face flushed. They were talking about their feelings and acknowledging that this was about to get complicated. And for all her pushing him to be brave, she was terrified. Of this. Of him. Of getting hurt if she decided she wanted to be brave again too.

But what was she afraid of, really? Now that she understood Finn, she trusted him. She had trusted him with her body last night, and today she knew she could trust him not to hurt her, because he wanted her. All of her. Everything that she brought to a relationship. He had seen the darkest, most fearful parts of her character and he hadn't flinched. The only thing that he had done that had made her mad was to give her the money to pursue her academic ambitions. It was hardly a capital crime. She calmed her breathing, felt her face gradually cool, and then threw down the gauntlet.

'So, what are we going to do about this?'

CHAPTER FOURTEEN

WHAT WERE THEY going to do about it? Right now, half his brain was voting enthusiastically for heading straight back upstairs, directly to his bedroom, saving the talking for later. They'd done pretty well communicating that way last night. But it had hardly made things less complicated.

What if Madeleine was right and he was holding back because he was scared? Was that who he wanted to be—someone who missed out on the thing that they desperately wanted because they weren't brave enough to take a risk?

And, God, did he want her. He had wondered yesterday if maybe this blinding lust was the result of a very long dry spell as much as it was about her—but he couldn't have been more wrong. He wanted her even more now than he had before and he couldn't imagine existing in a form that didn't want her. How had he thought that he could just walk away from feelings like that?

'You're right. I've been scared. I *am* scared. Divorcing Caro was the biggest knock to my upward trajectory since as far back as I remember. It floored me. And I was terrified that I was going to lose everything—that the business would fail and I would fail and it would be a slippery slope back into poverty.'

Madeleine watched him in silence, her expression serious as he looked for the words that would explain why he had taken so long to give in to the feelings that had been assaulting him since she had walked back into his life.

'And then you showed up and there was this connection between us and I knew it was something powerful. Something important. Something I knew I wouldn't want to stop, if it started.'

'Which is why you've been fighting it.'

'Yes. I mean, fighting it pretty ineffectually, but yes.'

'I think after last night we can agree neither of us did a great job at that.'

She smirked, and he felt it all the way in his gut. But he had been fighting it for a good reason. Because his life had fallen apart last year, and he had been scared in a way he hadn't felt since he was a kid. In a way he never wanted his own children to experience.

'I can't promise that if we try this it will work, Finn. There's no guarantee.'

'But you want to try?' he asked.

'Do you?'

God, why does this have to be so hard? Finn thought. *Why does it have to be so scary?*

He couldn't imagine contemplating this sort of risk for anyone but Madeleine. But, scary or not, he couldn't see how he could walk away now. He had fallen in too deep without even realising it. How could he walk away when he had had a taste of what it was to see someone and be seen? To have peeled away one another's fears and defences and looked one another in the eye, knowing that the only thing that would get in their way now was a lack of courage.

He knew that Madeleine had courage by the bucketful. She was the one that had brought them to this point. He didn't want to be another person who let her down.

'I don't need guarantees, Madeleine,' he said, examining his feelings, boiling it down to what really mattered. 'I just need you.'

She looked at him for a long moment. 'Why?'

He held her eye and knew exactly why she was asking. Knew how many times people had looked at Madeleine and assumed they could know everything about her by the way that she looked. He also guessed from the confidence in her posture right now and the hint of a smile at the corner of her mouth that she knew exactly how brilliant he thought she was. If she wanted to hear it out loud then he would tell her. He didn't want her to ever think that she had reason to doubt how he felt about her.

'Because you're brave. And determined. And fiercely independent. And you like my kids and we have the same taste in pizza. Because my home and my office and my life seem dull when you walk out of them.

Because last night was incredible in a way that I've never felt before. And yes, you're beautiful. You know I think that, but I hope you know how unimportant that is to me.'

The smile spread across her lips, upwards, to crease faint lines around her eyes.

He laughed, walking around the kitchen island, suddenly desperate to have her close. She turned on the spot, following him with her eyes as he came closer, until she had her back to the counter, leaning back on her elbows as he stopped in front of her. He could lean in now, take her lips with his and, if the previous night was anything to go by, he wouldn't have another coherent thought until morning. But he wasn't ready to lose his mind just yet. Not when his senses were so damn delighted with what was right in front of him. Madeleine settled into her lean against the counter and quirked an eyebrow at him. She was going to wait for him to come to her. Good. He wanted to drink her in a little. Soak in the promise and potential of this moment before they jumped in.

He rested a hand either side of her waist, trapping her against the counter, but he still didn't lean in. Not yet. Instead he looked at her—looked inside himself at the riot of sensations that she provoked in him. But at the centre was a stillness, and he knew without having to think about it what that meant. He lifted a hand to her jaw, his thumb following the path of her cheekbone, his fingertips settling in a sensitive spot behind her ear.

'Nice speech,' she said, her arms lifting to rest gently on his shoulders, her gaze flicking between his eyes and his lips.

'I'm not done yet,' he said when his lips were just a breath away from hers. 'I love you. And I'm going to want you for ever. I hope that's okay with you.'

He felt rather than saw her smile.

'I think I like the sound of that. Because I love you too, and I wasn't planning on letting you go.'

EPILOGUE

'BELLA! HART! GET back here!'

Madeleine sat with Jake, watching Finn and Josie chase after the twins as they headed for the garden gate, running with their cousins.

'Still time to change your mind,' Jake said with a smile, and Madeleine rolled her eyes.

'Just because you want to keep him all to yourself.'

'Are you kidding? He'll be at mine all the time once you're married. Anything to get away from the ball and chain.'

She hit her brother on the arm and relaxed back in her chair as she watched Finn trying to wrangle the kids back into the garden.

'Honestly, though, sis, I've never seen him happier. You either. It's good to have you back.'

She felt her eyebrows pinch as she looked at her brother. She hadn't even realised Jake had seen how sad she'd been for so many years. And wondered, not for the first time, just what he'd been hoping for when he'd sent her to stay at Finn's place. Stupid interfering brothers with their insight and good instincts.

'Yeah, well, I guess he's all right really.'

'I should hope so,' Finn said behind her, making her jump. 'Otherwise I'd have to ask them to take that marquee down.'

'And tell the two hundred guests to stay home,' Jake added.

'And send back the cake.'

'Enough, you two,' Madeleine said. 'God, what have I done?' She shook her head, laughing. 'I'm not returning the cake. Fine, I'll marry you, even though you're really annoying. But I'm uninviting Jake.'

'Deal,' Finn said, leaning in for a kiss.

'Gross.'

But Madeleine grabbed Jake's hand before he could walk off.

'Seriously, though, little brother. He's a good one, and I'm not sure I would have seen it if you hadn't dangled him in front of my nose for, you know, the last couple of decades. I love you, and I owe you.'

Jake pulled her in for a hug before holding her out at arm's length and taking a long look at her. 'You're welcome. I'll redeem my Brownie points in babysitting time. I'm just glad to see you both happy.'

Finn pulled her into his lap as they watched Jake go over to battle with the kids, all six of them, and he wrapped his arms tight around her waist.

'Did I mention that I love you?' Madeleine asked, turning her head to look up at Finn.

'Once or twice,' he replied with a smile, dropping a kiss on her nose. 'But I can probably stand to hear it again.'

'I love you,' she said again, her voice turning serious. 'And I'm going to stand in front of all of those people tomorrow and tell them. But really, as long as you know, nothing else matters.'

'I know,' he said, bringing up a hand to cup her face, brushing a kiss high on her cheekbone. 'The same way that you know that I love you. More than I ever thought possible.'

She turned to watch Jake and the kids, the marquee for her wedding set up for the morning, her whole future playing out in the garden of their new home.

'I'm so glad you were brave,' she told Finn, and he pulled her in a little tighter. 'When I was out on that ledge, hoping that you were going to come for me.'

'How could I not be when you'd shown me how it was done?' he said softly into her ear.

* * * * *

If you enjoyed this story,
check out these other great reads from
Ellie Darkins

Falling Again for Her Island Fling
Surprise Baby for the Heir
Conveniently Engaged to the Boss
Falling for the Rebel Heiress

All available now!